THE

AGREEMENT

J.C. REED

&

JACKIE STEELE

An Indecent Proposal: The Agreement

Copyright © 2015 J.C. Reed & Jackie Steele

All rights reserved.

Cover art by Larissa Klein

Editing by Shannon Wolfman

ISBN: 1519799233
ISBN-13: 978-1519799234

THE AGREEMENT

Predictable. Boring. Safe.

That's what life is supposed to be like. As the rightful heir to Waterfront Shore, I would gladly refuse my inheritance. I don't want the money. I sure don't want to have anything to do with its dark past. Except for the letters of my deceased mother, I would be willing to cut losses and move on and give up my rich lifestyle. But my stepfather expects me to marry. And then there is my new fiancé.

My hot, fake fiancé.

Tall, handsome, mysterious.

That's how Chase Wright is.

Unfortunately, he is not mine.

Unfortunately, too, the day I hired him, I signed an agreement.

When an innocent plan lands us engaged, none of us are prepared for the consequences. No one warned us that we could fall in love. Maybe The Agreement wasn't such a good idea.

I should stay away from him and forget about our one night together.

Except he doesn't want to...

PROLOGUE

The first time I saw Lauren Hanson, it was on a snapshot in a thick folder brought to me by my lawyer, Richard Crook. I was sat at the mahogany desk in my multimillion-dollar mansion on the outskirts of Santa Barbara in California. The valley stretching beyond the large bay windows was streaked in the colors of the setting sun—the deep red as ominous as the rage surging through me at the prospect of what I was about to do.

Laurie was an attractive girl with brown hair reaching down to her narrow waist—the kind you could twist around your fist and pull gently as you rode her hard, then forget all about her. She looked like a nice girl with an innocent glint in her hazel eyes that reflected even through a photograph. In less than forty-eight hours I'd be using that innocence to make her mine forever.

"Are you sure, Mr. Wright?" Crook asked.

I nodded gravely and tossed the folder back to him.

"You've barely looked at her," he continued, "or her background. Maybe you should wait. I could look into alternatives and—"

"I'm not interested in her life story," I said through gritted teeth, cutting him off. "Just make that meeting happen, and I'll take over from there."

Crook heaved a defeated sigh. He didn't argue as he picked up the folder but left Laurie's photo on the desk. Her hazel gaze looked at me accusingly. I turned it over so I could flee it for the time being, figuring soon enough I'd have no choice but to face the hatred embedded in her eyes, staining her heart forever.

"Tomorrow afternoon," Crook said upon leaving. "If you change your mind…"

"I won't," I said sharply, "and don't be late."

Chapter 1

It was almost noon when I arrived at my apartment. Everything was silent when I entered. After insisting for an hour that Chase take me home—the one place I had always felt safe but no longer did—he had given in, but only under the condition that I called him immediately if anything scared me. The moment I closed the door behind me, Jude called over from the kitchen, "Where have you been?"

I shrugged out of my jacket and joined her at the kitchen table. "I spent the night with Chase."

Her mouth dropped open. "You did what?" She let out a cascade of incredulous laughter.

"It wasn't what your dirty mind is imagining." Actually, it probably wasn't far from the truth, but Jude didn't need to know that. In spite of the situation, a laugh escaped my throat.

"What happened?" Her eyes were as big as saucepans, and her smile was so bright I wouldn't have been surprised if a satellite could have picked it up from the stratosphere. But as much as I wanted to tell her, I couldn't spill the beans because I had more pressing issues to worry about. Ever since I had opened the envelope, and seeing Chase's and my face circled with a thick red marker, I felt a kind of foreboding that left me nauseated. Chase had been right when he asked me not to tell anyone about it. Jude might be my best friend, but I didn't want my fear to infect her and risk her getting all paranoid on me. My paranoia was enough to deal with. Having her fears imposed on me was the last thing I needed.

"I'm sorry for dashing your hopes, but I didn't sleep with him," I said.

"Oh." She stared at me in badly disguised disbelief, the disappointment clearly etched across her face. Eventually, she shrugged her shoulders and a grin tugged at her lips. "What's wrong with you? You spent the night at his place. It would have been so easy, Laurie."

"I'm not sleeping with him, Jude. Period." I glared at her, my gaze both imploring and threatening if she didn't drop the subject. "He's just a friend and that's all I want him to be."

Which was a lie.

A big, fat lie.

I could see her doubt.

And then her phone rang, and I breathed out a sigh of relief.

"Whatever. You're making a mistake waiting for Mr. Prince," she muttered, and walked back to the living room, closing the door behind her. I sighed again, then put my keys on the table and squeezed out of my shoes. Seconds later, a scream echoed down the hall.

"Jude, are you okay?" I dashed for the kitchen.

"I'm going to be a TV personality," Jude squealed as soon as I opened the door, her voice echoing off the walls.

I put my handbag on the kitchen table and squeezed out of my shoes as I took a moment to digest the news. Why was she going to be a TV personality? And then I remembered her mentioning a blog and a TV channel being interested in giving her a prime spot.

Her face appeared around the corner before I had the chance to reply. "Did you hear me?"

"I think all our neighbors did." I smiled at her. "What happened?"

"Oh God, I can't even believe I'm saying this, but I just talked to some big-shot producers and they told me I'm going to be a TV personality. For real."

"Tell me all about it." I pulled her to the couch with me,

forcing her to sit down as I tucked my legs beneath me. "What did they say exactly?"

"You know the blog I told you about? The one with my personal home-decorating ideas?" I nodded and she continued, "Well, apparently, it was a huge success with the focus group, and now the head honcho of the channel wants me not only to appear on a huge network once a week, but he's also asked me to do a show. That's two regular gigs!" She held up two fingers and began to squeal. "Can you imagine?"

"Two shows?" I asked.

"Yes."

"Wow." I shook my head in admiration. "That's amazing." Drawing her in for a tight hug, I wrapped my arms around her, letting her happiness pour through her into me. "Congratulations. Now you'll have to hire me as your personal bodyguard to keep them from wanting a piece of you once you're famous." Smiling, I grabbed her in another hug, mostly to stop her from jumping up and down, which she always did when she was excited. She had both the excitement and the attention of a five-year-old— things that often came in handy, like now that I needed to take my thoughts off the hot guy who had proposed.

"Tell me everything. When are you starting? How much are they paying you?" I squinted, unable to remember whether she had said anything about a paycheck. "They are paying you, right?"

She nodded. "Plus insurance and a bonus if I reach a ten per cent increase in viewers. I also get a personal assistant and a driver who picks me up and drops me off at the studios."

"Wow." I couldn't help but be impressed. I had never envied people working in show business because, first of all, it required a certain amount of self-confidence. And second, a chatty personality, which I didn't possess. Public speaking had always come naturally to Jude. Back in college, she wouldn't hesitate to stand up in front of a class and start asking questions. She had always been popular. As she often said, she loved the attention. She loved to inspire people, which was why she started blogging in the first place. Even then I knew she had the potential to be huge one day. Me...not so much. I always took things quieter, maybe because all my life I had tried to remain hidden. Low-key. Inconspicuous.

"See, the thing is I'm supposed to have my first day tomorrow. Just a test shooting to see how people react to me and whether I have what it takes." She laughed nervously. "I'm not sure I have what it takes to impress them. At home, behind the computer screen, I feel like I can be myself. But in front of a huge crew, and recorded live? I don't know, Laurie."

"You do have what it takes. I have no doubt about it," I

said, meaning every word of it. "If anyone can impress them, it's you, Jude."

"Thanks." She shrugged, her nervousness slowly dissipating. She was going with the flow, living in the moment, worrying about things when she was forced to face them—the way only Jude could. "I was wondering if I could borrow something from your wardrobe." Her red-tinted lips stretched into a wide smile—the kind she always employed to get what she wanted. I didn't mind sharing whatever I had with her, but Jude *never* borrowed my clothes. My taste in clothes and consequent wardrobe were the two things she always laughed about.

"Why? What's wrong with your clothes?" I asked warily.

"Nothing." Her voice came out too loud. She sounded so guilty I almost cringed. "I just like yours better."

Big, fat lie.

She never ever would wear my clothes unless…

"Oh my gosh." I snorted. "Admit it, Jude, your clothes are too slutty for the occasion."

"They're not."

I crossed my arms over my chest and regarded her, amused. "Look who needs one of *my* business blazers now. After all those years of insulting my choice of clothing, I should make you write an apology letter." A better idea crossed my mind. "In fact, you can choose whatever you want under one condition. You wear something from my

10

wardrobe for a week. And yes, it has to be a different outfit every day."

"No." Jude's eyes widened in horror. I bit back a snarky remark. My clothes weren't *that* bad. "They just called to remind me to wear something conservative. As in a dark gray suit with just a hint of color." She said the word like it was a rash. "I have no choice or say in the matter."

"And now you want to borrow my stuff?" She looked so horrified I could barely contain my laughter. Jude wasn't just keen on decorating homes, she also liked to do it dressed up like a sexy goddess.

"Take whatever you want. I'm happy you get this chance. You've worked so hard, you deserve it."

"Thank you. I wasn't sure how you'd react, which is why I've made you dinner."

I gawked at her, only now smelling the faint scent of roasted onions and something else. I sniffed the air loudly as I fought to place the smell. "What is that?" It wasn't unpleasant, just…strange.

"I told you, dinner," Jude said.

"You never cook." Which was the equivalent of 'you can't cook'. Neither Jude nor I had a chef bone in our body.

"Yeah." She grimaced. "I found out the hard way when I had to ask the neighbor to help me figure out the oven. His name is Tinker. As in Tinkerbell."

I raised one eyebrow. "Honestly? You want me to

11

believe we have a neighbor by the name of Tinker?"

She shook her head and winked.

"Okay. If you have to know, I don't remember his name. But look, I'm telling you the truth." She walked into the kitchen, expecting me to follow her, which I did. "I'm not a completely lost cause, which is why I've tried my hand at a foolproof recipe passed on to me by my grandmother."

And by that she meant Google, because Jude's parents migrated from Australia to the States when she was an infant and she never got to meet her grandparents.

"What's this?" I looked at the sticky, boiling brown mass and fought the urge to grimace.

"It's vegetables." She looked at it. "You know, that stuff that's supposed to be healthy and good for you."

The gooey stuff looked like no healthy stuff I had ever seen.

I grinned. "In that case, I'm starving."

"Then wait until you see the meat." I stared at her open-mouthed as she opened the oven, wondering what she meant by that.

***

Jude's first attempt at magic, a.k.a. cooking, looked edible. An hour later, a mouth-watering scent wafted over from the crispy brown roast beef with roast vegetables.

"Want some?" Jude said, coaxing me proudly.

Everything looked so delicious my stomach made a growling sound in response. "Pile it on, darling."

She chuckled and retrieved her carving knife, which we had never used in the three years we had been roommates. Jude plunged the knife into our dinner, only it barely penetrated the skin.

"Are you sure this is ready?" I asked skeptically. "Isn't the meat supposed to be tender?"

"I followed the recipe down to a T." She frowned at it as she managed to cut a piece of sinewy meat. "Maybe it's supposed to be a steak."

No steak I had ever seen resembled *that*.

Ah, but the trouble with recipes was that they were written by people who *knew* what they were talking about, and as a result they believed the whole world did, too.

***

It took fifteen minutes and our entire strength to cut the meat in two thin slices. We were sitting at the table, our plates in front of us, eyeing the brown, palm-sized cuts warily.

"You did this for me, and I'll gladly eat all of it," I said resolutely, pointing my fork to my dinner plate. "It looks delicious. I'll give you that."

"It's a Thai recipe. I used fresh spices," Jude said flatly.

"Really?"

She nodded.

"Wow. A Thai recipe." I nodded, impressed, and pushed a tiny piece of meat into my mouth. "Your grandma really knew how to cook."

Oh, God.

It was hot. So hot, I stopped chewing and scanned the table for anything to drink.

My eyes started to water as the burning sensation in my mouth began to grow. How much spice did Jude pour in there? A whole bottle of chili?

I coughed.

"Is it too hot?" Jude asked, worried.

"No. It's perfect." I shook my head and wiped at the tears trickling down my face. I didn't know what was worse: the burning in my mouth or the way the spices made my eyes and nose water. Or the fact that I had no idea how to tell her that her cooking truly and utterly sucked. Big time. Through my foggy vision, I watched Jude take a bite and immediately stop chewing. Her eyes popped wide open and red splotches dotted her cheeks as she began to wave her hands in front of her mouth.

I laughed. She looked like a dragon about to spit fire.

"You should have said something," she whispered in mortification.

"What? And spoil seeing the look on your face?" I laughed again. "No way. Besides, it's not *that* bad."

It was worse than anything I had ever tried in my life. Counting the fact that Jude and I had been roommates for years, that said a lot about just how bad it was.

"I'm not eating it. And neither are you." She snatched away my plate before I could pretend to want to take another bite.

"I'm so sorry. This cooking thing isn't for me. I swear this is going to be my last attempt ever." She shot me a hesitant smile, and I nodded even though she had made that same promise so many times before, I had lost count. "Ready to order pizza?"

"Are you sure? Maybe once it's cooled down…" I trailed off.

To be honest, I couldn't wait to see her concoction safely tucked in the bin, but the beauty of friendship is you don't hurt each other's feelings. And so I settled on telling a little white lie, which wasn't really that much of a lie, because, if I focused hard enough and imagined myself in a nice restaurant, Jude's meal almost tasted bearable.

Jude shook her head decisively. "No. I'm ordering pizza."

Thank God!

How could I argue with so much determination?

"If that's what you want. The gesture's all that counts." I

handed her the phone and watched her speed-dial. As she turned away I snapped a quick picture of her cooking disaster on my phone, figuring a scrapbook was the perfect Christmas gift. She'd be both mortified and laughing her head off at the same time. And it would be the best reminder never to try Thai again.

Chapter 2

"Chase wants to do what?" Jude asked, chewing on her slice of pizza.

In spite of the clouds of disbelief floating around inside my brain, I laughed at Jude's shocked expression.

"He said he'll marry me. Before my birthday."

"Without having sex first?" Jude asked incredulously.

I nodded.

She leaned back, still regarding me. "Wow. Who would have thought he was so old-fashioned? He strikes me more of a 'wham bam, thank you, ma'am' kind of guy."

The truth was…I had thought that, too.

"Is he religious?" Jude's voice penetrated my thoughts.

"Not as far as I know." I shook my head. "He does it to

help me, not because he's in love or really feeling it."

"And you said?" Her expression changed from shock to delight as she drew out the words. I didn't need to see her sudden grin to know what answer she *expected* me to give.

"I said—" I stopped, hesitating. Yesterday the though of marrying Chase had been appealing, but in the morning, during the drive home, I realized that pulling Chase into the midst of the mess that was my life might not be such a good idea. Not when I wasn't sure who had sent the envelope. I didn't like Clint watching us, nor the fact that Chase could end up hurt. The previous day's decision had been a rash and foolish one. Away from him, his stunning eyes, and the magnetism he exuded, I knew better than to let myself fall into the fairy tale attitude that there might be something between us. Besides, marriage is sacred—a bond between two people, pursued out of love, not out of need to get something I had always wanted.

"Laurie?" Jude's voice drew me back in.

"Obviously, I'll have to give it more thought and—" I brushed my fingers through my knotted hair, faintly aware of the fact that *if* I was to marry Chase, I'd have to schedule an appointment with a hairdresser and find a dress and…

Oh, God.

I was officially crazy, because no woman in her right mind would marry a stranger. Not even one as hot as Chase, especially not after the previous night and relentless memories of his tongue between my legs, licking me, filling me with want and need for his hard body. I pressed my legs together, my mind fighting to suppress the haunting images before my eyes. But I was so turned on, I wouldn't have been surprised if it was written across my forehead.

"I can't believe it," Jude said, jerking me out of my thoughts. "You're getting married, and then you and Chase will end up having lots of babies and I'll be Auntie Jude."

"No." I slapped her arm gently before she got completely carried away and started choosing baby names. I had thought hard about it and eventually came to the conclusion that the shorter we kept the entire experience, the better. "I'm not *really* getting married, Jude. It would be a fake marriage that would lead to a fake divorce. I wouldn't stay married to him."

Her delighted smile disappeared. "Why not?"

"Because." I threw my hands up in despair. "There are a million reasons. Like the fact that we know literally nothing about each other."

"You're using 'literally' in the wrong context, sweetie. Technically, you know more than nothing about him, like his name and how he earns his living. Then there's his age."

Which was true. And I also knew the tattoo hidden behind his tight shirt. The way he slept. The way he kissed. What he tasted like.

Oh, God.

Why wouldn't those naughty thoughts ever stop torturing me?

"I got it," I said, irritated.

"Did you really?" Jude asked, eyes glinting with humor.

"Yes." I rolled my eyes. "The point is, marriage is a huge commitment. Every second couple is getting divorced, and even if this isn't your usual love relationship, I don't want my future to be marked by it."

I winced inwardly as I realized how I sounded.

Why was I even bothered by the fact that Chase and I might get a divorce one day in the near future when it was nothing but a business proposition anyway?

"I mean, who wants a woman who couldn't even stay married for a year?" I added. "It's a bad stigma, like running away from the altar, or ditching someone for your job. I don't want to add 'unstable' to my almost nonexistent relationship résumé. Same for him. I don't want to jeopardize his future and ruin the chance of him meeting 'the one.'"

Even as I said the words, my throat choked up. Eventually, he would meet 'the one' and then I'd be completely out of his system.

The thought sucked. It made me furious, both with him and with myself for thinking it.

What was wrong with me? Chase didn't belong to me, so the feeling of jealousy came out of nowhere.

"May I remind you he's the answer to your prayers, Hanson?" Jude whispered. "This could all be a sign. In fact, I'm pretty sure it's meant to be."

"A sign of what?" I asked warily.

"Of bigger things to come."

I stared at her. "Seriously? Do you really believe in that stuff?"

"I do. Let me take out my astrology chart and give you a few pointers." She grinned.

"That's interesting. Next thing I know you'll be reading my future."

She sat up, tucking her legs beneath her. "Okay, what's his sign?"

"I was being sarcastic, Jude," I muttered, adding, "Besides, I don't know."

"Well, ask him." She pushed my cell phone across the table.

"I can't just call him."

"Why not?"

I threw my hands up again in exasperation. "Because—" My brain failed to come up with a plausible reason. Chase had insisted that I call him anytime—only, people said things like that all the time without actually meaning them.

Jude raised her brows. "Come on. You really need to know the significant stuff."

I laughed out loud. Knowing his astrological sign was

21

hardly significant. In fact, it couldn't be more trivial.

"Fine. I'll text him." With Jude peeking over my shoulder, my fingers flew over the touchscreen buttons as I typed the message.

What's your sign? In case you ask, Jude wants to compile a personality chart, even though I'm strictly against it. Don't ask. I didn't know she was psychic either.

I pressed the send button before I could change my mind and put the cell phone aside because it wasn't important. Even *if* Chase and I married, I didn't need to know anything about him. In fact, I even muted the sound so I wouldn't read his reply straight away.

Jude regarded me with an amused smile on her face.

"What?" I asked, irritated.

She shook her head, all fake innocence. "Nothing."

Unfortunately, 'nothing' was never really nothing with Jude. A few moments later, the screen lit up with a reply.

I'm a Taurus. Very passionate lover who enjoys giving and taking in equal measures. If you open up your heart, I'll treasure it forever while carrying you on the wings of passion.

Jude giggled. "He's so hot."

"I can't believe you're falling for this crap." I switched

off my phone and pushed it across the table. "Obviously, he looked it up on Google and now he's feeding us what he thinks we want to hear. He's such a player."

Wings of passion?

Make it more like wings of his fingers.

I drew a shallow breath as I remembered the way his exploring fingers almost broke my self-control.

For crying out loud.

I had almost slept with the guy. Now, in broad daylight and with him at a safe distance, I was happy I hadn't gone through with it, because who knew…maybe he would have changed his mind about marrying me once he got the cream, proverbially speaking.

"He's probably slept with thousands of women," I added, not least to convince myself that men like Chase came with a big, fat 'player' sign scribbled all over their face and private parts.

"Maybe, but experience is sexy in a guy," Jude said, still grinning.

Experience?

The guy probably had a little black book containing all the names of his conquests plus pictures so he could remember them all. If we walked into any bar in L.A. he'd probably know half the female clientele. The fact that he drove me to a stranded bar so far out of the city for our initial interview proved that point. The female population he hadn't fucked was probably diminishing by the day, and I was one of the few remaining closed-legged women he had left to chase.

Come to think of it, my legs hadn't exactly stayed closed, either.

I slumped against the cushions and rubbed a hand over my hip where his fingers had dug into my skin to bring my core closer to his talented tongue.

After twenty-two years of staying out of a man's bed, even I hadn't been able to resist him.

Men like him should come with a warning: danger to your panties.

"Aren't you going to reply?" Jude asked.

"Sure." I sighed, focusing my mind on what to write. Eventually, I typed up a message, then showed it to Jude.

I'm an Aries and I'm very much into the whole BDMS thing. In fact, why don't you send over your ego right now so I can kick its ass before it can fly away on its wings of passion.

Jude laughed. "You're a lost cause."

"I try." I shrugged and took a deep breath, my mood dimming as the stack of opened letters on my desk caught my eye—all reminders of my failure.

"No job yet, huh?" Jude said, following my line of vision.

I shook my head. "Not even the slightest hint of interest. Just one rejection after another. I'm overqualified for most normal jobs and not qualified enough for anything related to my degree."

It was so frustrating, I felt like hitting a wall.

"You could always start your own business."

"With what money, Jude? Every business needs investment. Besides, what could I possibly be doing?"

"I don't know." She fell silent for a moment and her forehead creased in concentration. "You have a phone, so you could offer a phone service, you know, people call in and ask for your opinion."

Not bad…if only it were realistic and could actually make money. And then there was another problem.

Google.

"What sort of opinion?"

"I don't know." She shrugged. "They could call and ask you for the time in Alaska."

"What a fantastic idea. I'll be able to pay the rent in no time," I said, struggling to keep my sarcasm in check. "And then I would never have to be lonely again, because between you and me, it must be heaven to have your phone ringing at the most unfortunate hours, and you get to chat to all the creeps in the world. Really, sometimes I have no idea how you come up with all those crazy plans of yours."

Jude's expression darkened instantly. "At least one of us

can pay the bills, you know."

I could tell she was pissed by her rigid stance. "I didn't mean—"

"If you started blogging like me, and actually invested some time rather than giving up so easily, then your work might actually get you somewhere," Jude said.

Ouch.

"I'm sorry," I said, ready to back off, because she was right. Jude was the most inventive person I knew, and probably the most capable. She always persevered, and when one plan didn't pan out, the next one was already waiting around the corner. She had started almost fifty blogs and worked her ass off trying to hook advertising companies before she found success with one. For that, she deserved more than just my respect.

"I can't do that," I whispered. "What you do, blogging…it's amazing, but I don't have that gift, Jude. It's not something you learn."

She heaved a long sigh. "I was just trying to help you. It doesn't have to be what I'm doing."

"I know." I wrapped my arms around her and pulled her close. "Thank you for watching out for me." My voice broke at the realization that she was the only one who did. She was the only thing I had left in the world. While Chase seemed to be around now, it had been Jude who brought him into my life in the first place. It had been her who made the impossible possible. For a change, I wanted to do something nice for her.

"Let me take you out." I jumped up and pulled her to her feet.

"No, Laurie."

"I insist." The fleeting thought of a maxed-out credit card entered my mind and left it just as quickly. I wasn't much of a drinker, and wherever Jude appeared, guys offered to pay. Some even forked out a drink or two on me in the hope to impress her with their display of so-called generosity. The whole evening wouldn't cost me more than forty bucks. A hundred, tops. A few dollars, more or less, wouldn't really make much difference to my overexerted bank account. And to be honest, I really owed her.

"Maybe tomorrow."

Judging from the way she kept fidgeting with the hem of her shirt, she wanted to come. She wanted it badly; she just felt guilty at the prospect of letting me pay.

"Clint has left me some money. We might as well spend it." The half-lie made it past my lips so fast, I barely had time to acknowledge it.

Yes, Clint had insisted I cash in my allowance check, but it was for life-threatening emergencies only. Besides, I wasn't comfortable taking money from him. He was already too involved in my life, always lecturing me on the merits of dedication and hard work. I didn't want to give him the satisfaction of admitting that my attempts at attaining financial independence had remained fruitless and would most likely stay that way for a long time.

"In that case—"

I didn't catch the rest because Jude was already out the door, and halfway across the hall, heading for her bedroom. I followed and watched her through the open door as she chose two outfits for us—dresses so short I knew I'd end up tempted to wear a long coat just to hide my half-bared ass. Maybe Jude didn't mind flashing her panties to anyone who wanted a glimpse, but it wasn't really my thing having other people staring up my legs.

I was ready to tell her just that when she tossed a piece of fabric my way and glared in case I started an argument with her.

For once, I clamped my mouth shut and just did as she expected of me.

Chapter 3

Five minutes into our drink at Jude's favorite bar and already there was a line of interested guys, all eyeing up her long, toned legs and devastatingly low cleavage. She had it all: slender, tall body, hair and skin to die for, and the charm to enchant an entire room with just a modest smile. But I wasn't envious, because being a male magnet had a huge downside to it.

"Did the guy just grope me?" she whispered, pointing at the grinning man in the adjacent cubicle. He was half sitting, half leaning toward Jude, his naked arm almost resting on the back of Jude's chair, his fingers brushing suggestively over the polished wood. He winked at me, knowing we were talking about him, and leaned forward, ready to commence whatever he thought was his game, when I turned my back on him.

"Talk about creepy." I rolled my eyes and agreed to swap seats with her even though I knew it wouldn't stop his ogling, or the next brainless ape, who thought every attractive woman was an easy catch.

The bar was full, as usual. The chatter of conversations intermingled with the background music. We were at Jude's usual table, which the bartender had cleared the moment she had entered the door.

"I can't believe you're getting married," Jude said. "I feel like a mother bird whose baby's leaving the nest, flying into the unknown. I'll have to teach you everything I know about the birds and the bees."

I laughed at the twinkling in her eyes. "There's not going to be any of that, because Chase and I aren't interested in consummating the marriage."

Her brows shot up. "So you've decided to marry him?"

Dammit! Why did she have this uncanny ability to coax people into revealing their plans and decisions before they even knew for sure what those plans and decisions were?

"I don't know," I said. "My head tells me that it's a stupid idea. It's all so definite and scary."

"It probably is…for a commitment phobe, like you." Her blue eyes narrowed on me.

"I don't suffer from commitment phobia."

"And you want me to believe you?" She regarded me with raised eyebrows. "There are sexy guys and there are good, nice guys. And then there's a mixture of both."

"Let me guess, Chase belongs to the last category," I said, and raised my brows. "Your point being?"

"My point being he's a rare breed. A catch." She smiled. "In all honesty, what keeps you back, Laurie? Life doesn't have to be as difficult as you make it out to be. It's hard, and cutting, full of mistakes and failures, but once you've reached the top, with the sky so low you can almost touch it, and the whole world at your feet, it's beautiful and exhilarating. You'll see it's worth the ride."

"Full of mistakes and failures? Where's the beauty in that?" I joked, smirking.

"You know there's beauty in everything. You're just not looking hard enough. So…what do you *really* want?" Jude asked.

I regarded her, surprised by the sudden determined edge in her voice. "You know what I want."

She shook her head. "No, I don't know. At some point I thought it was obvious, but not anymore. You've been talking about those letters for years. Now here's your chance to go after them, to uncover the truth and find peace once and for all. It's most certainly your last chance, Laurie. You said so yourself. And yet here you are, hesitating, suddenly afraid. All my effort to help you has been in vain."

"Nothing's been in vain. By me getting engaged, Clint got the point that I'm not after his money. I'm no threat, but I'm also not afraid," I whispered.

Or was I?

She leaned over the table and squeezed my hand, her warmth seeping into my skin. "Then just do it, get what you want, and then move on with your life. It's not like you're pressuring him. He wants to do it. He's made his choice. Now you need to make yours. It's about time you leave the past behind."

That was easier said than done when it kept staring in your face day in, day out. Jude didn't understand what I had risked to break free and get away. Getting married to receive my mother's letters would mean that I might end up diving back into the past, where danger lurked. Clint was a powerful man with many connections and dangerous friends. The letters might provide all the answers I'd sought for years, but they could be answers I might not like. The truth was I wasn't sure if I was really ready to know all the secrets that had plagued my mother. The last months with her—her vacant expression, the angry outbursts followed by fits of crying—still haunted my dreams. I dreaded the letters would not help me eradicate the past, but rather strengthen my fears and suspicions.

"Laurie," Jude whispered. "Remember you're not alone.

I'll always be here to help you, and I'm sure Chase won't let you down. Sometimes the hardest lesson to learn is not to fight whatever's coming your way. Get the letters and see what happens. For all you know, maybe your mom just wanted to tell you how much she loved you and she could only do so on paper. You need them for yourself to find out what she wanted you to know."

Nodding slowly, I buried my gaze in my cocktail glass, watching the bubbles slowly dissolving.

Refusing to marry Chase would be stupid. All my hopes, my dreams, my wish to be free of guilt, would dissolve into thin air, just like the bubbles in my glass.

She was right, as usual. Chase had offered his help, and he was making it so easy for me. I had already told Clint about our engagement. The first few steps were done, and Clint was now spying on us to find out if we were determined to carry out the wedding part. I took a deep breath and let it out slowly. If we didn't consummate the marriage, it could be annulled in less than twenty-four hours after I got my hands on the letters. Chase would be free and so would I—the only reminder of our time together a piece of paper that stated our marriage was void.

Why was I still hesitating, then?

Because you don't want to take advantage.

I sucked in my breath and held it for a moment. Sure, I didn't want to use him for my benefit, but there was

33

something else. The realization hit me so hard, I forgot to breathe.

Ever since the day we spent at the cottage, I could feel something fluttering inside me. It wasn't love. It was something else—something I couldn't explain.

It was deep and dark, like a current.

I wanted him.

To be mine.

I wanted him to like me the way I liked him.

Not just sexually, but on a personal level.

I swallowed the lump down my throat as I realized that the more I resisted Chase, the more I ended up liking him. And not in a way I could easily deal with.

My heart lurched in my chest at the thought of him.

I liked him too much—so much that I was way past friendship territory. The idea of him becoming my husband was a dangerous path to my heart, particularly because he could never be.

Already I was having trouble keeping my emotions in check around him, and we had barely met. What would it be like being near him all the time while having to deal with my naughty thoughts on a daily basis? To resist his flirtations, his random touches, which didn't seem to be so random after all.

"I'll be right back," I said, and grabbed my handbag, heading for the restroom—away from Jude's probing glances, relentless questions, and anything else that might just send my thoughts circling back to him.

Running away, as usual.

Inclining my head, I stared at my reflection in the mirror, not quite liking what I saw. My skin had a hue of pale gray to it, the bags under my eyes too pronounced in the harsh neon light. Thank God for foundation and bronzing powder, because I looked like shit and felt even worse. Maybe I'd be able to hide the way I looked, but how could I possibly make a secret out of the fact that, on a mental level, I knew I was biting off more than I could chew? Chase was a sexual guy, no doubt about that. If the way he so easily had swayed my mind and tempted me to sleep with him was any indication of our future interchange, I was doomed from the start to give in to his wants.

Judging from his confidence, he was used to getting what he wanted, and he had admitted that he wanted me. There was no doubt that he'd try to get me into his bed again. Only, now I wasn't stupid enough to believe I could resist him, nor was I stupid enough to believe that my heart wouldn't get involved along the way.

But Jude was right: I needed the letters to finally find closure.

So many years had passed; so many phases of depression had made me beg for such an opportunity as this. But falling in love with Chase wasn't an option. I knew that if he pushed hard enough, I'd be all sugar and butter again. And then, in the heat of the moment, I'd open my heart, my soul, my body for him, and he'd crush it along the way. I couldn't afford that. I couldn't let our relationship progress.

I stopped in my thoughts and my breath hitched in my throat.

What relationship?

We had none, at least not in the traditional sense, I reminded myself. The few dates and a bit of flirting meant nothing.

Nothing at all.

"I'll just have to keep my legs crossed and closed. How hard can it be?" I muttered. I had only practiced abstinence for the last twenty-two years, never trusting a guy enough to get physically and emotionally involved.

"Depends on who he is."

I turned and shot the woman behind me a shy smile, realizing I must have spoken out loud and she must have heard it.

She was dressed in a blue dress that built a strong contrast to her red hair pinned high over her head and the thick layer of pink lipstick. Her whole attitude screamed confidence and something else I couldn't quite pinpoint. "There's good sex and there's bad sex," she continued as she inspected herself in the mirror, smacking her lips in the process. "If he looks clean, listens to you, and takes good care of you, he might be well worth it."

As she peered at me from under long, fake lashes, I realized what she was oozing.

Life experience.

"Probably," I whispered. With a last glance at her, I headed out into a narrow hall, eager to return to Jude and finally get back home.

Only, as I scanned the crowded bar, she was nowhere to be seen. My glance swept over the busy tables and clientele, but Jude wasn't among them. She must have met someone. There was only one person who'd know. With a sigh, I strolled to the bar and motioned the bartender to get his attention.

"G'day, Laurie." He smiled, revealing his perfect white teeth. "What can I do for you?"

"James." I shot the familiar face a bright grin. James was a good friend—a sexy, tanned Australian, who Jude would have dated, were it not for him playing for the other team.

Not that she hadn't tried anyway.

"Have you seen Jude?"

His eyes brushed over the room and the tiniest hint of a frown appeared on his otherwise smooth forehead. "I saw her a few minutes ago heading outside, probably for a smoke."

"Thanks." I was about to turn and go looking for her,

when James called after me.

"Hey, Laurie. How's your job search coming along?"

"Still nothing. They don't want to hire graduates unless they work for free." I smirked. "So I might as well do a few unpaid internships. If only I'd get one without having to move, because in NYC they're basically all snapped up for the next five years."

He nodded, his eyes lit up with sympathy. "Well, if you need a job, feel free to ask us. We have an open position coming up. It's yours if you want it."

I looked at him, smiling. "Thanks. I appreciate the offer, but—" I hesitated. Could I really afford to decline?

For months I had spent hours and days looking for a job related to my degree—without any success. If I didn't find anything soon, I'd end up in serious financial trouble, and I couldn't afford falling into an even deeper financial hole, seeing that I had already maxed out all my credit cards. "Maybe. I will give it some thought and I'll get back to you, okay?"

"Sure." He returned my smile and winked. "See you around."

"Yeah." I headed back for the hall, which was now crowded with people making out. At the end of the narrow space was a backdoor that led into an alley, which I knew Jude usually used for smoking a cigarette whenever she went out. I opened it and walked outside. The door closed behind me as I scanned the dark space.

There was no sight of her. Sighing, I breathed in the cool night air, which wasn't too bad by L.A. standards, and gripped the doorknob, ready to head back into the bar, then pushed.

I frowned when the door didn't open.

Shoot.

I had locked myself out.

Chapter 4

I stared at the door, willing somebody to open it. Blaring music echoed from inside so loud, I doubted anyone would hear my pounding. Even though I knew my attempts would remain futile, I tried one last time and then gave up in favor of a different approach. To re-enter the bar, I figured I had no other choice but to walk around the block. It would take me five—ten minutes, tops. It wasn't a big deal at all, except...

Alleys of east Downtown Los Angeles scared the shit out of me, especially now that I was on my own and surrounded by darkness. Garbage littered the sidewalk, large bins blocked the view, and the lack of street lamps made it a place of anyone's nightmares. I didn't mind the smell or the rats scurrying around, or the few syringes and condoms lying around. Never mind some of the burned-out buildings or the scary sub-art culture with graffiti adorning the walls that screamed 'stay the fuck away,' but the fact that those dark alleyways were a sign of rebellion on their own—a place neither courageous people, which I wasn't part of, nor the police would venture into at night, unless they had no choice.

East Downtown L.A. was a city of chaos, where shady deals were made, and people were killed or fought for their life—where everything dark poured out of the beauty of L.A. and was swept into a place that screamed danger and poverty. Some said it was a gateway to hell—out of the view of the rich and famous, stacked away from the tourists. A place where superficial beauty surrounded a perilous sliver.

Ever since moving to L.A., I had known to stay away from those uncharted back lots of downtown at night. Generally safe at day, L.A. was different in the darkness, especially the Seventh to Ninth Street, when the poor homeless and the addicts started crowding in some places, while others, being territories belonging to the gangs that ruled them, became deserted.

My eyes scanned the long, narrow alley stretching to both sides of the backdoor. A stray breeze blew my hair into the face. I was brushing it away when thudding footsteps echoed from my left. My head snapped toward the noise, my eyes wide, my heart racing in my ears.

A naked bulb over the door cast an ominous light, its weak rays barely reaching the large bins on my left side, filled to the brim with garbage.

I swallowed the lump in my throat and pressed my hand against my pounding heart as the steps inched closer. The figure of a guy entered my line of vision. Even in the darkness I could make out the dull eyes, hollowed cheeks, and clothes that had seen better days. He looked like a drug addict in dire need of the next quick fix. Or maybe he was already high out of his mind, seeing that he barely acknowledged me as he passed me, each step slow and steady, and then he was gone. I breathed a sigh of relief and hurried in the direction he had come from.

Wrapping my arms tightly around me, I quickened my steps. I had almost reached the end of the alley when steps echoed behind me. With a quick glance over my shoulder, I kept walking, but my breath caught in my throat. Someone reached me in a few strides—a different guy, and yet he seemed familiar. My mind raked through the last hour's faces but didn't come close to finding an answer.

"Hey," a voice shouted close to my ear.

Shit. Shit.

My breath came fast as my steps hastened in the hope I could get out of there as fast as possible.

The possibility of screaming for help entered my mind, but I quickly discarded of it. Even if someone heard me, I knew no one would come to my aid.

"Hey, you," the guy yelled again. "I'm talking to you."

His hurried steps told me his pace had picked up, the knowledge making me panic so much that I started to run.

But it was too late.

He grabbed my shoulder and twirled me around.

"Hey, you." He cocked his head, and I recognized a guy I had seen eyeing up Jude earlier. "Where's your friend?"

By friend he was talking about Jude.

"She went home," I whispered in the hope he'd leave us both alone.

"So it's just you?"

My breath caught in my throat as I stared at him. Why the fuck had I just given him that answer? The streets were abandoned. We were alone and I had just told him that.

"Actually, she's waiting for me." I pointed to the left. "Along with our friends," I added. "They're all here. Sorry, I gotta go so we can make it to the next party. It's quite a drive from here."

I shrugged my right shoulder, hoping he would let go of me, while my heart lurched in my chest like crazy.

Instead of letting go, his grip tightened. "Not honest, are you?" His voice carried the telltale slur of a drunk, his tone accusatory. The real danger was never the east Downtown alleyways themselves, I realized. It was being paid attention by the wrong guys—the ones psycho enough not to understand that their attention was unwanted.

"How about we spent a little time together?" As if to make his point unmistakable, his hand began to rub my shoulder a little harder than necessary.

My pulse raced so hard it was almost impossible to formulate one clear thought.

"We could meet up tomorrow," I heard myself saying— the one thing I hoped would help me get rid of him. "I'll give you my number and we can arrange something." I squeezed a hint of cheeriness into my voice to mask the underlying fear that threatened to seep out of me.

"All right." The guy looked at me suspiciously, then retrieved a piece of napkin with a pen out of his pocket. "What's your number?"

I gave him the wrong number, of course, silently praying that the tremor in my voice wouldn't give me away. As I was about to turn away from him, his grip on me tightened while his other hand fished his phone out of his pocket. Paralyzed, I watched him dial the number I had given him. Someone replied almost instantly.

Someone who clearly wasn't me.

"Thought so," the guy mumbled, his smile smug.

Slowly, he pushed his phone back into his pocket, his eyes boring into me with a hint of danger. "Trying to wriggle out of this, bitch?"

My voice failing me, I swallowed hard and shook my head.

"Think you can play me?" His voice carried a hurricane of anger. "Let me make one thing clear, bitch. Nobody messes with me. And especially not bitches like you."

I shrank back. "No, I must have gotten it wrong. Let me try again and I'll—"

My voice broke as I considered my next move.

The moment he'd pull out the paper, I'd try to run, if only he'd let go of me.

"Doesn't matter now. What's the purpose when you're already here?" he cut in before I could continue. "You're my bitch and I won't let you go until you give me what you promised."

"What? I didn't promise anything."

"You seduced me." His lips curved into a knowing smile. "Sluts like you always like to be fucked. I know the kind of girl you are, Laurie."

His words made me flinch. "How do you know my name?" I asked, shocked, my legs trembling and my breath coming shallow as a shudder ran down my spine.

"Let's say I eavesdropped on you and your friend." He smiled again, shaking his head in disapproval. "Marrying a guy just to get some letters. I bet you're a gold digger, out for his money."

45

I stared at him. Of course he must have picked that up from our conversation and created his own story in his twisted mind.

"That's right. My fiancé is rich. In fact, one of the richest men around here," I heard myself saying, hoping that this would infuse some fear into him. "And if you don't let me go now, you'll be sorry."

He let out a loud laugh. "So, where is he?" He turned his head left and right in mock curiosity. "Probably in his castle, asleep, while his whore fucks the next guy." He grabbed my hair and pulled my head back. As he leaned forward, his breath coming hard, it took every ounce of me not to faint from the pain searing my scalp.

"Don't worry, Laurie. I won't spill your secrets. I won't tell anyone of your little affairs." His hand slid down my front and reached my skirt, lifting it up roughly.

Shit.

This wasn't happening.

Why had I listened to Jude and changed into a dress of her choice? Underneath it, I wore only a pair of skimpy panties, and those barely covered my private parts.

My fingers clutched around his hand before he could move it between my legs.

"Let me go," I whispered, angry with myself for getting into this kind of situation. My angry command was only rewarded with him laughing. He was obviously enjoying the

46

situation as it was, which just confirmed my earlier suspicion that the guy was a psycho. And judging by his roaming hands, probably someone who was capable of doing more than just harassing a young woman in an empty alley.

"Get your dirty hands off me," I hissed.

"Or what, huh?" His smile turned into a grimace as his fingers tangled in my hair, pulling harder, until the pain in my scalp turned into a nasty burn.

My hands fumbled in my bag for the Mace I always carried around.

"You'll give me what you're good at, bitch."

My fingers finally wrapped around the tiny bottle. My heart pounding hard in my chest, I pulled it out, ready to use it, but he slammed it out of my hand. The bottle landed on the hard concrete floor somewhere to my left, obscured by the darkness. But the sudden noise was enough to distract him. For a moment he let go of me, and I used the opportunity to turn around and head for the main road. I was almost out of the alley when strong arms gripped me, dragging me behind the large bin. I screamed as loudly as I could, but the sound came out all muffled and choked by his hands pressing against my mouth.

"Fucking bitch." With a hard thrust, he flung me onto the hard ground.

I caught my fall but scraped my knee in the process, the

pang of pain knocking the breath out of my lungs. Turning around, I stared at him, fear washing over me in thick waves as he leaned over me and opened his belt. "For that you'll pay."

"Please, no," I whispered, my voice choked with fear. I tried to scramble to my feet but he positioned his boot in the middle of my chest, pinning me to the spot.

"You stay here, bitch." He used his belt to tie me up, a demonic expression on his face.

He was turned on, I realized. By my fear, by the thought of hurting me, the thought of being in control. As he kneeled down, between my legs, I started to kick and fight, and my voice finally found its way out of my throat.

His grip on my thighs was rough; the hands holding me down unyielding. His breath smelled of cigarettes and vodka, but that wasn't the worst. I could sense his intentions and my impending doom.

No one would hear my screams.

And even if they did, people were too scared in those dark alleys. No one would put their life at risk to help a stranger. With rising horror, I watched him unzip his pants. But he never got round to fulfilling his plans.

Two hands settled on his shoulders, yanking him away from me.

My rescuer's face was bathed in the darkness cast by his hoodie as he grabbed my attacker by his collar and kicked him so hard in the gut, I almost felt the impact. As my attacker lurched forward to fight back, the guy slammed his fist into his side. My attacker collapsed instantly to the ground, gasping for air, and then he stumbled to his feet, shaking badly.

"Shit." He groaned, the choked sound louder than his voice. "Shit."

I stared at the hooded guy dressed in a casual sweater, afraid to whisper my thanks; not quite daring to hope the worst was over. One of them could still pull a gun and the situation would escalate.

Hooded guy stepped toward me, his hand extending. I eyed his outstretched fingers warily, unsure whether to let him help me up, because I couldn't see his face.

Couldn't trust him.

"You okay?" His voice was deep and dark, carrying not even the slightest hint of fear.

His voice seemed familiar.

My heart began to beat frantically in my chest the way it always did when he so much as said my name.

"Chase?" I asked incredulously. My pulse raced so hard it almost drowned out my voice in my ears.

Of all the people in L.A., it couldn't possibly be him.

My rescuer pulled back the hood, exposing the gray-blue eyes that seemed to see right through me whenever he looked at me.

Oh my God.

It was really him.

"Why are you—" *Here*, I wanted to ask, relief streaming through me.

"Get up, Laurie. We don't have time. We need to get away before he gets help," he whispered, his gaze scanning our surroundings. Not out of fear, I was sure of that.

Help? I wanted to ask. The guy had attacked *me*, not the other way around.

But instead, I let Chase lift me up to my feet and half tug, half carry me out of the alley, and back to the main street, toward a midsized sedan I had never seen before.

It wasn't the same car he usually drove to pick me up.

"Is this yours?" I asked.

"Get in." Ignoring my question, Chase opened the door and motioned me impatiently to jump into the passenger seat.

Chapter 5

We sat in silence as Chase drove. Half an hour must have passed and yet my legs were still trembling. But at least my heart had stopped racing at some point. As we came to a halt at an intersection, I finally turned my head to regard Chase and noticed his rigid stance and the pallor of his face accentuated by the faint shadows beneath his eyes. He turned to shoot me a thin smile but the glint in his eyes didn't escape me.

Desperation.

Fear.

Something else.

Something darker.

Something I didn't want to see.

Whatever it was, I had no time to ask, because the lights changed to green and Chase floored the accelerator and the engine roared to life. I slumped into the comfortable seat, chewing on my lip.

Something was bothering him.

It wasn't just the way the worry lines between his eyes deepened that made me think that. His jaw was clenched, too, and his hands gripped the wheel so hard I could see the paleness of knuckles shining through his skin. Finally he turned his head to me and our eyes met for a second, but his expression was enough to make me brace myself for what was to come.

"What the fuck were you doing out there, Laurie?" he asked, his voice so low I could have almost missed the hint of anger in it. I looked at him, stunned.

Chase had never been angry with me before.

Wow.

He sounded so sexy when he called my name that for a second I forgot to reply. He turned his gaze to the street ahead and then back to regard me, and his sexy eyebrows shot up questioningly.

"I'm sorry. I didn't know I was supposed to ask for your permission before venturing out at night." I crossed my arms over my chest. "I'll make a note to keep that in mind next time."

"That's not what I meant," he growled, and rubbed his

face with his hand before slamming it back on the steering wheel. "Jesus, Laurie. Do you know what could have happened back there? You should never ever be alone on those streets."

I shot him a venomous look. How dare he try to make me feel guilty?

"It wasn't my fault, you know?" I said. "The door closed behind me and I couldn't get back inside."

"The guy was about to rape you," Chase continued, stating the obvious, probably not hearing a word I'd just said. "He was so fucking close to hurting you, to…"

He broke off, unable to finish his train of thought, but there was no need. The memories of the guy's grip on me, his hands on my legs, his putrid breath in my face, feeling his intentions even before he had unzipped his pants, would surely haunt me for the rest of my life.

I closed my eyes to stop the disturbing images running like a movie inside my head. For a few moments, I was rendered unable to reply. The silence felt oppressing, but truth be told I had no idea what to say to him. Incidents like that weren't supposed to happen. He wasn't supposed to have witnessed what was one of the most petrifying incidents of my life, and yet I couldn't be more thankful for his presence at the right time.

That I got myself into such situation made me feel shame and guilt, even though I knew it really hadn't been my fault.

"What were you doing there?" I repeated his question, unable to process the fact that he had rescued me. Of all the people in the world, and all the places he could have possibly been, he was there, in a tiny alley, at the time of my attack.

At the right time.

At the right place.

Like fate. Except my life had been so rough, at some point I had stopped believing in something greater.

Fate didn't exist.

"Chase?" I prompted when he didn't answer straight away.

"Shouldn't you just be happy that I was?" His gaze remained glued to the street ahead, his features a hard mask unbroken by emotion.

"Were you following me?" I asked, ignoring him.

"What?" He shook his head slowly and frowned. "Jude texted and invited me to join you. Said something about the evening needing at least a guy, so I came as quickly as I could."

"Oh my God. Jude," I whispered, as I realized I had forgotten all about her. "I have to go back to her. She's probably waiting for me."

"No, Laurie." His frown turned into a scowl. "I don't think that bar's the right place for you. Text her to tell her you're with me."

I hesitated.

He was right, of course. If I went back, there was the slight chance that the guy was waiting for me, ready to get revenge for Chase kicking him. No, make that a big probability. Only this time, I was sure the guy's friends would jump in to help.

Shuddering, I grabbed my phone, then texted Jude that Chase had picked me up. I also instructed her to get home safely, leaving out my little incident, and then stashed the phone back inside my handbag.

I knew I could never go back to that place, and I'd have to explain to Jude what happened at one of her favorite bars. And to think, I had even considered applying for a job there, desperate to make some cash, even though the area code should have been reason enough to stay clear off it. Sooner or later something would have happened, and Chase might not have been there to help me.

I had been so close to being raped.

The thought struck me with full force.

"You're right. I shouldn't have been out there alone," I whispered at last, not even daring to look at Chase as the truth escaped my mouth. "I can't thank you enough for coming." My voice sounded choked, trembling. "You saved my life, Chase."

For a few moments we remained silent. The car slowed

down and eventually came to a halt. I could feel Chase's gaze on me. Eventually his hand touched my face, his fingertips tracing the contours of my chin.

"When I saw you on the ground with that guy on top of you, you scared me. I thought I was too late." He cupped my face into his hands, forcing me to look at him. "I'm just glad nothing else happened. That's all I'm saying. And I want you to know that I won't let anything like that ever happen to you again."

My breath hitched. He made it sound like we had a future. Like he'd always take care of me. Jude's words popped into my mind.

Relationship material.

As I gazed at him, my blood rushing in my veins, I braced myself for his kiss. He was so close I could feel his breath on me. I opened my mouth slightly—welcoming, inviting him. Chase looked up from my lips to my eyes, hesitating.

Ruining the moment.

"Do you know what you want?" he asked, and let go of my hand.

For a moment, I just stared at him. Had I spoken my thoughts out loud? Startled, I closed my mouth, my cheeks burning. His eyes narrowed on me questioningly, and a smile lit up his face. "I can park somewhere until you decide."

My gaze traveled from him to the fast food restaurant on the left side, where cars waited in line to communicate their orders via speakers and drive-thru windows. That was when the meaning of his words dawned on me.

Both disappointment and relief whipped through me.

Obviously, I couldn't have him realize just how much I wanted his body. But, for some reason, I almost wished he knew, so we could do something about it.

"No, it's all right." I eyed the restaurant. I had been there a couple of times during my college years, and while it wasn't my favorite place, the food was delicious. "I'll take the double-double animal style with fries."

"Drink?"

That was a no-brainer. "Vanilla milkshake, if they have one. What about you?"

"The same." He smiled as he headed for the drive-thru. We ordered our food, then, after repeated insistence, Chase let me pay and picked up our order.

"It appears we like the same food," he said, and handed me the vanilla milkshake. "That's the second thing we have in common. There's also a third."

I knew it was an attempt at easing the tension between us. And it worked, because I felt compelled to ask, "What's the third?" I recalled his words. "We're both in love with independence, and we like the same food. What else do we have in common?"

He tilted his head and narrowed his eyes in that incredulous 'You don't know?' look.

"We both like it when I eat out." His lips twitched. I stared at him, not comprehending the meaning of his words...until the naughty raise of his brows and glint in his eyes gave him away.

I almost choked on my drink. Surely he didn't mean what I was thinking. And then his perfect lips turned into a lopsided grin.

Oh, God.

"You know why I like the taste of anything sweet?" Chase asked. "It reminds me of you, and it makes me wonder what you taste like today."

"Won't happen," I said, mortified. "Last time was a mistake. You got lucky. It was a one-off mistake."

"I doubt it. You were very much into it, as far as I remember. It's only a matter of time until you'll want it again. I bet you've already thought about it."

He was right, as usual.

I tried hard to think of a snarky remark, but, as usual around him, my brain eluded me.

I turned away, pressing my lips into a tight line to hide my smile. Who knew chemical reactions could be so strong? Whatever he said or did, Chase always seemed to bring a grin to my lips, even when he wasn't even trying. As much as I wanted to push him away and keep both my physical and emotional distance, it wasn't possible. Not when he was around. Not with those dimples I adored. Not when he touched me the way he did with his eyes and his hands, as if he somehow knew what to do to stir the kind of emotions in me no other man had invoked before.

My stomach growled, reminding me that we hadn't eaten yet. We were back on the highway now. Only this time I had no clue where Chase was taking us. Even though I was hungry, I couldn't just tuck into my food. I decided to wait until he stopped somewhere.

"Where are we going?" I asked casually when he took the exit onto Interstate 405 toward Sacramento.

"I'm taking you to a special place for a special meal. Just wait and see." He gave me a short glance, and then his eyes were back on the road. "But if you'd rather not, we could stop somewhere and take a break."

"No, it's okay," I said casually. "Surprise me."

For a few minutes, silence ensued. Chase took another exit, and I decided I couldn't take the thoughts in my head anymore and asked him to switch the music on. As a soft-rock ballad blared through the speakers, I tuned out, my mind focusing on the curvy road that separated the cars from the side of a cliff with just the tiniest bit of old and rickety guardrail. My heart pounded as the bends came and passed, some sharp, others hidden—all of them frightening. My fingers curled around the soft leather of my seat, and several times I found myself gasping for air.

Chase didn't seem particularly fazed.

"You should keep your eyes closed," he said, his hand briefly squeezing mine for assurance.

"Please keep both of your hands on the wheel," I said, which was rewarded with a laugh.

"Relax, Laurie. I know this place. There's nothing to worry about."

"He said before he crashed and burned." I smirked.

"Tell me," Chase said, ignoring my comment. "Why did you ask for my sign?" It was a means to divert my attention, for which I was thankful.

I closed my eyes and begged my racing pulse to slow down. "I didn't. It was Jude who wanted to know."

"Speaking of signs and meanings. Do you know what Laurie means?" he asked.

I opened my eyes, eyeing him, my curiosity awakened, the road momentarily forgotten. "No idea. Maybe you'll enlighten me."

"Laurie originates from the Laurel plant that was used as a crown to symbolize victory in ancient times. It's a symbol for honor and prize."

"Right." I smirked again. "So I'm a prize."

He laughed, the tinkling sound igniting something inside me. "Maybe. Who wouldn't want to be some treasured prize?"

"Says the guy who likes to do the chasing." I grinned at him.

"A prize to chase," Chase added meaningfully. "Laurie and Chase. The two words fit. Don't you think?"

My heart began to hammer hard. I opened my mouth to reply when the car slowed down, then the engine died.

"Here we are." He pulled the key out of the ignition. "Technically, the parking lot is closed at night, but no one's here to check on us. It's a good place for privacy, you know, if you wanted to enjoy a meal."

I could hear the undertone in his voice. He was definitely not talking about food, but for once something outshined his sexual innuendos.

I peered out the windshield and my jaw dropped. Stretched out in front of us was Los Angeles, lighting up the night sky. For a second I felt overwhelmed.

It was so beautiful I slowly sucked in my breath and held it. Thousands of lights scattered across the city, shimmering like Christmas lights on a tree. The black sky looked like a canvas with millions of stars glinting brightly, creating a scenic view worthy of a blockbuster movie.

It was, in one word—breathtaking.

"Wow," I whispered, and stepped out of the car, completely immersed in the view before me. "You should charge for sightseeing."

A soft wind blew my hair into my face. Chase reached

me and gently pulled my hair back.

"Maybe I'll do that someday, if my income sources ever dry out. You've really never have been here?"

I shook my head. It had been in L.A. for three years, but I wasn't quite the explorer, so never really ventured into unknown territory—similar to my sexual life. "Don't start. I *know* I've been missing out."

He shook his head. "No, I don't think that's it. You've just been waiting for the right person to show you the view."

I looked at him silently. In the darkness under the stars, surrounded by glimmering lights, he was beautiful, his lips kissable, and his breath intoxicating.

So close I could call him mine.

Mine.

My mouth went dry at the thought. I opened my mouth to reply when he leaned into me, his hot lips lowering onto mine. And then he kissed me, his hands roaming over my body, fingers squeezing beneath my clothes, all in front of the city—as if we were the only people in the world. His tongue dipped in and out of me, tangling with mine, leaving me in want. I moved my hands around the back of his neck, eager to deepen the kiss, but he pulled back, leaving me in a daze.

I almost asked him not to stop.

But only almost.

Frowning, I watched him walk back to the car and get the fast food bags, before reclaiming his place next to me.

"I promised you a date with a meal," he said. "I can't let my girl starve."

His girl.

My heart fluttered.

"Usually, dates are overrated." I grabbed my handbag. "But this...I think it's the best date I ever had."

"Well, we still have plenty of dates left, and I still have a few tricks up my sleeves, so don't get too impressed too easily."

"You've been counting?" I asked, surprised.

"Aren't you?" He smiled coyly. I stared at the tiny dimple in his cheek like an idiot.

God, he was so beautiful, it took my breath away...and something else.

My inhibitions.

My wish to keep the honey pot sealed when all I could think of was the fire he'd ignite in me if I only let him have it.

"Maybe." I had been counting more than just our dates. Like the times he had smiled at me and made my heart flutter.

For a while, we ate in silence, enjoying the view. The city was so beautiful, I felt like with every breath I inhaled a bit of that beauty.

"Do you drive a lot, Chase?" I asked eventually, turning to face him.

"Yeah. Why?" He stopped eating and regarded me with a strange expression on his face. I shrugged and turned away, but I could feel his prodding gaze on me.

"You seem to know L.A. pretty well. That's all."

He gave a short laugh. "When I'm chasing after gigs, I'm on the road all the time. Heading from one audition to another can get lonely and boring." He shrugged and leaned back. "It makes a nice change having you around, Laurie."

Why the heck did he sound so serious and sincere?

I swallowed hard. My head began to spin just a little bit.

Careful now.

I already had a hard time keeping a cool head around him. If I let him, he'd say something that would melt my reservations.

"You're right. It's a special place. In fact, I think it's the most beautiful place in L.A."

"Yeah." He nodded, his electric eyes boring into me. "But it's only beautiful when shared, and I'm happy it's you I get to spend this moment with."

He looked at me, and once more, my breath stopped at his words, at how much I wished them to be true.

Embarrassed by my stupid thoughts, I turned away and began to fumble with my food to keep my hands occupied.

His fingertips began to caress the back of my neck, then

traveled down my spine. My skin began to tingle and a slow pull settled within my core.

He was the most beautiful person I had ever met, but also the most frightening.

I'd have to tell him.

Soon.

Lay out the cards in the open.

And watch him walk away.

Because falling in love with him was not an option.

Chapter 6

"Chase," I whispered, unwilling to pull my hand out of his. How could I explain that he couldn't keep doing the things he did? That I was afraid of falling in love with him? That his words made my heart flutter and carved my stony heart into a form that only had room for him? That I both wanted to and feared breaking our moment? That I wished he would hold me forever, but at the same time, I hoped he'd just leave.

He was the kind of temptation I couldn't resist.

The kind of seduction from which I would never return whole.

"Yeah?" He turned his head, his eyes liquid puddles in the night.

I opened my mouth but no words came to my mind, except that I wanted to kiss him again, to touch him, to feel his lips on my skin. My physical hunger was gone, but inside I was starving for him. His touch had left so much desire I could feel it between my legs. A longing to experience things with him again, explore more of what he had to offer, tap in to the unknown. To make him mine like no other man had been. But for that I had to share my body with him, gather the experience I didn't possess.

I couldn't just ask him if he wanted to try it again, could I?

Stepping in front of him, I let my hands trail down his shirt. I rose on my toes and began to kiss his neck because I couldn't reach his mouth. A shaky breath escaped his lips, as I let my fingers trail deeper and guided them beneath his shirt. Unlike the first guy who had dared to touch me, Chase was all hard, defined abs and taut skin. In the darkness, his eyes sparkled like dark sapphires. Under my lips I could feel his warm skin and the rhythmical throbbing of his pulse. My fingers went lower until I reached the telltale bulge inside his jeans. With hesitation, my palm pressed against his entire length with just enough pressure to feel him stiffen.

"Laurie," he whispered, slightly choked. "This isn't the right place. It's not how I envision your first time."

My fingers froze, but I didn't remove my hand from

him. "You've been imagining my first time?"

"A couple of times, yeah." He laughed, his voice low and hoarse, trembling with desire. "And if you keep doing that, I don't think I'll be able to control myself for much longer."

"Maybe I don't want you to," I whispered.

"What are you saying?"

Instead of replying, I began to stroke and rub gently with my fingers, but rhythmically until I could feel him getting bigger. Harder. It pleased me to get a reaction from him. It pleased me to see that I could turn him on—that he was hard for me. He groaned, and his lips found my neck. For a moment I thought I had him right where I wanted him, but then he pulled back and pressed his hand against mine, stopping my motion.

"I don't think you know what you're doing." His voice was still low and hoarse, but there was a dangerous undertone to it.

"I don't think you know what I want." I shrugged and looked at him, all wide-eyed innocence. "Maybe you're right, and I need you to teach me."

He tilted his head, eyeing me up and down. "You did that on purpose. Get me hooked so I'd have no choice but to teach you. Clever move." His lips curved upwards. "Fine, baby. Let's have it your way."

He opened the car door and pressed me onto the

backseat, then settled between my legs. It was an awkward position, the space too confined, too uncomfortable. But in that instant it couldn't have been more perfect. Once the door closed, he switched off the lights and turned to me with a grin.

"You're too hot for your own sake, Laurie."

The hoarse tone in his voice sent a blazing heat as hot as a raging fire through my body. I lay back and watched him trail his fingers up my legs, rekindling the fire he had ignited. "I don't think you know the effect you have on me or what you make me want to do to you."

Whatever he wanted, I wanted. I wanted to know. To experience. To find out why we had that intense chemistry.

My heart began to hammer hard against my chest as he leaned over me, full of hunger, and let his hand slowly trail over my face, over my breasts and my hips. I sucked my lower lip into my mouth, watching him, silently urging him to move faster.

Before I knew it, he pulled off my panties with a speed and agility I never thought was possible for such a tall guy.

He leaned back, watching me for a while, a sexy, lazy grin on his face.

"What?" I asked. The warm air whipped against my exposed flesh, and a deep shudder ran through me.

"You're even more beautiful outside than under the covers." His hands lifted my legs up, and his fingers spread my lips wide apart.

I had no idea why…until his fingers began to slide up and down, grazing my clit, rubbing my sensitive flesh, spreading the moisture that seemed to pour out of me.

Holy heaven.

What was happening to me?

Chase's touch sent another whiplash of fire through me. His fingers were determined, but there was something gentle about his movements. He kissed me one more time, setting me alight, and then his mouth settled on my core, his tongue trailing between my damp folds.

Biting my lip hard, I leaned back and enjoyed his hands doing the magic, though to be honest, I thought Chase was magic himself. His palm massaged my entrance while he began to suck, and his breath caressing my most private parts. I moaned in delight as he continued to drive me closer to the edge, silently urging me to take all that he could give. Chase had an extraordinarily talented mouth. Even his breath turned me on. If he continued the way he did, I knew I'd fall apart. It wasn't a question or possibly. It was a fact.

"You have the most beautiful pearl in the world," he whispered in his sexy, deep voice. "A tasty pearl with the scent and warmth of vanilla."

His breath came heavy as he plunged the tip of his finger into me—but not deep enough; he was not yet willing to give me the full release.

"This is what it feels like to have one bit of me inside you. Imagine what it'd feel like to take me in, inch by inch." He pushed his finger into me, all the way in, and then began to thrust.

Oh, God.

My heartbeat sped up.

It was so much and yet so little.

My legs stiffened as he pushed in and out of me with a precision that made me gasp and had me moaning in pure ecstasy. I bit on my lip in agony. *Please.* I needed to fall. Something needed to shatter, I just didn't know what. Only that I felt myself slowly letting go of the rope I had been holding on to for years. The rope that had kept me away from men like him.

"Please, Chase," I whispered. "I'm ready. I want to do it with you."

But Chase didn't seem to listen. His rhythm picked up in speed, harder and faster, as he ignored my desperate pleas. My mouth opened to ask again, but his thrusts and his tongue pushed my body over the edge. Thousands of feelings washed over me. My body convulsed, and I fell apart, feeling like I was being driven out of the darkness and right into the light. The waves of an orgasm rocked me, each more fulfilling than the other, leaving me completely drained.

This was it.

My first orgasm with somebody else. Only it had not been just one, but two or three orgasms in a row. With nothing but his lips and his finger inside me.

The realization that Chase had caused it hit me fast. As if sensing my thoughts, Chase laughed, satisfied, proud.

"I can't give you more, Laurie. Not today." His breath came low and raspy, and yet his eyes looked at me amused. For a moment, the most raucous of thoughts raced through my head. Chase had said he'd only sleep with me if I made the first step. With renewed attention, I sat up.

"Lean back," I whispered. Without waiting for his reply, my hands busied themselves with his jeans. Slowly at first, full of hesitation, I unzipped them and pulled them down over the generous bulge, freeing his erection.

For a moment I stared at it, unsure what to think or what to do. I looked up at him.

"What do you think you're doing?" He exhaled slowly, watching me, taking in my reaction.

"I don't know," I whispered. "Giving back, I guess."

"No." He shook his head, but the expression in his hooded eyes told a different story.

"Why not? You had your fun. Now it's my turn."

"Laurie." He hesitated, fighting with himself. "Just because I'm giving doesn't mean you have to give back."

"It's all right." I smiled. "I want to learn anyway. Now's

72

as good a time as any."

For a long moment, Chase watched me but remained still. He didn't have to speak his consent. His eyes were dark and glittering with desire. There was no doubt how much he wanted me to. How much he needed me. There was no doubt I wanted to pleasure him as much as he had pleasured me. Our eyes remained locked while I somehow managed to move between his strong thighs, sinking to my knees in front of his imposing swell.

Only...

Somehow I didn't imagine it to be so big.

It pulsated with authority—bursting alive with energy. It beckoned me, making me wonder if it was as hard as it looked.

A gasp of shock escaped my mouth as my fingers touched his swollen shaft. It was so firm and yet soft—like a sword in his sheath. And long. I doubted I could fit his entire length inside me. His finger was one thing, but this—the monstrosity that seemed to fascinate me—I wasn't sure I was ready for it. It scared me, by standing proud and tall and sturdy. My breathing came out labored as my gaze brushed up and down his swollen shaft, anticipation and curiosity gripping me.

"I don't know what to do," I whispered, letting my hands trail up his considerable length only to rest at the hard, round crown. My body vibrated, and moisture gathered between my legs at the idea of tasting him, taking him all in.

"Teach me, Chase." It wasn't a plea; it was a demand.

"I'm not sure about that." He looked so pained that I kept wondering if I had hurt him somehow. Or was his need causing him physical pain? I had no idea. But the way he continued to shiver, coupled with his scent and his sexy sounds still echoing in my head, made me want him even more, if only to please him and see him unravel the way I just had.

"But I want to," I whispered, more solemn now. "Teach me, Chase."

"There's no secret, Laurie. You just have to…" He paused, considering his next words. "Just suck like you did those grapes."

I looked up, stunned, wondering if that was the reason he had stared at me full of fascination when I ate the grapes. It didn't even occur to me that he might be thinking of sex at that time while I had been wondering if he was attracted to me.

Talk about a poker face. I could most definitely learn a thing or two from him.

"But this isn't a good idea. It's not the right place," Chase continued.

He was lying. Maybe his voice and his mind were doubtful, but his body knew exactly what he wanted. And he needed it now—I could feel it in his erection pulsating in my hands. I pushed him down, pushing up on his thighs, as I leaned forward.

Ever so slowly, I lowered my mouth on the sensitive crown, kissing it gently, and a low groan escaped from his throat. I placed my lips around him, cupping the tip, and began to suck. Gently at first, surprised by the salty taste, and then harder, as I let my mouth and tongue play up and down his length.

"God, Laurie." He moaned. Inside my mouth I felt him grow bigger and thicker, as if that was even possible, making it hard to take him all in.

He started to tremble and his breath became rasped, gasping. I had no idea that I could bring him so much pleasure, but the thought pleased me, encouraging me to go as far as I could, and then push some more.

Chase clasped his hand around mine and guided me to grasp his full erection, tightening my grip, showing me how to move my hand up and down. He groaned again, and in the moonlight he opened his eyes to watch my every movement, his mouth slightly open, his beautiful eyes dark and hooded.

Our gazes locked, and my breath hitched in my throat at the fire burning in his eyes. It made me want to suck harder, to swirl my tongue faster until he leaned back against the seat, his erection slick and magnificent.

Tightening my grip around him, I moved my hand faster, which seemed to make him breathe harder.

"Christ," he whispered, and begged me to stop while his thighs began to quiver. He was coming. Hard. He didn't have to tell me. I knew it because I could feel his tension. The thought turned me on. The knowledge that I could bring him so much pleasure made me wet, because now I knew that not only did he have the power to bring me the pleasure and gratification I needed, I had the power to let him fall apart.

"No, Laurie," he whispered shakily. When I didn't stop, he pulled out of my mouth. "I'm going to come."

He made it sound like a bad thing.

I looked up confused, unsure if I was hurting him, even though that did seem like a far-fetched idea. I had done what I had been told. Until now he had seemed to enjoy himself.

His face was flushed, and his breathing came hard. His thighs were still trembling, and his erection pulsed so hard that I was sure I could make him come if he just let me.

"Fuck, you're good," he whispered, his face a mask of pleasure and surprise.

Why was he surprised?

I had no idea. I simply did what he had told me. What felt right.

"I'm good?" I smiled.

As if sensing my attempt to go for it again, he glared at me, and then he adjusted his jeans before I could change my mind. "But you're not ready."

"I am. I want to do this." I let my hands trail back down his thighs, but his fingers clasped around my hand, stopping me.

"No, Laurie. Not now."

Oh God, I had never seen so much passion in his eyes. So much contradiction. And self-control. He wanted to rip off my clothes and get it done there and then, and yet I could see the hesitation, the desire, the fear. I could see it all. And yet he didn't let me finish what I had started. Didn't let me have the pleasure of seeing him come, like he did it with me. The thought made me so angry I stormed out of the car, slamming the door behind me. My pulse was racing. Inside I was fuming. If he had just let me, I could have given him pleasure.

I balled my hands to fists as I stared at the horizon, ignoring his presence behind me.

"What stopped you?" I asked, staring at the sky, not even trying to hide the disappointment oozing from my voice.

"You," he whispered. "I don't want to hurt you." He placed a finger beneath my chin and lifted it up, forcing me to meet his gaze. "I like you too much, Laurie. What you did, touching me, taking me into your mouth"—he paused—"it's a sure way to make me lose control. I don't want that until I know for sure that you're ready and that we have the right place."

Slowly, he leaned forward, kissing me, wrapping his arms around me until my anger began to ebb away.

"All right," I whispered, my heart beating frantically against my chest. "Let's do it today. At your place."

He didn't reply. Did he even hear my suggestion?

I searched his gaze and frowned. He seemed distracted, his eyes alert and his body tense.

"We have to go." His voice carried a hint of urgency. "A patrol car's coming."

I followed his line of vision toward the road, but Chase motioned me to return to the front seat.

"What about my panties?" I scanned the floor in search for them, unsure how I could have misplaced them. My mind was a complete mess.

"Leave them. We have no time, Laurie."

"Okay," I said, straightening my clothes. Within seconds I was back in the front passenger seat. Chase started the engine, then pulled back onto the highway. Like predicted, an LAPD patrol car drove past, but we were already back on the road and picking up speed.

"I feel like I'm fifteen all over again." He laughed, eyeing me sideways.

"You did things like these at fifteen?"

He shrugged, as though that was supposed to explain everything. "I'm a guy."

And a sexy one at that. I bet the girls in high school were all over him. Someone like him probably had many women lining up. And judging from the mirrors in his bedroom and his talented tongue, lots of experience.

As if he sensed my thoughts, his hand touched mine. "What, Laurie?"

"Nothing," I whispered, which was kind of a lie. To admit what I was thinking, that I felt jealousy at the thought of him having others, was wrong. I had no right to feel that way. Chase might have been the first who touched me and taught me how to pleasure a man, but he didn't belong to me.

"You look tired," Chase whispered. "I'm taking you home."

I opened my mouth to protest but stopped. Maybe it was for the better.

"Sure. It's late anyway," I said, having a hard time controlling the disappointment pouring through me. It didn't make sense. Why did I want to please him so much just because he had changed my mind about sex?

Because you enjoyed it, Hanson, and you want him.

Stupid, stupid mind.

I shook my head, annoyed with myself.

Chapter 7

Throughout the ride Chase entertained me with stories about all the things he had experienced in his career as an actor. I listened, half interested and half distracted by the longing inside me.

The car came to a screeching halt outside the apartment building. A look at my watch told me it was almost three a.m. The lights in Jude's bedroom were out. She was most certainly at home, and would be great company even if I woke her in the middle of the night. Yet I could barely bring myself to leave Chase—the one person who had made me feel so confused about our sexual encounter. I wanted to get down and dirty with him, if only to stifle the heat inside me. So, naturally, I wondered how Chase could remain so composed and easygoing, as if nothing had happened between us.

"Here we are," Chase said.

"Thanks for tonight." I avoided his gaze, not sure whether I was thankful for him saving me, or the time we had together.

"I enjoyed my time with you." His voice was low, his tone filled with the usual undercurrents implying so much more than he'd just said.

"So did I."

For a moment silence ensued. It was bearable, almost welcome. I scanned the dark windows of our building. Everyone was either tucked in for the night, or had gone out. Except for the faint noise of traffic carrying over, everything was quiet. If we waited up an hour, Chase and I could watch the sunrise. Only I wasn't sure I could just sit there, without touching him, without begging him to take me back to his apartment. I almost dreaded entering my empty bedroom and getting engulfed in the thoughts I knew would start off like this:

Did I do something wrong that made him pull away? Was I making a mistake by wanting to get involved with him? When had my feelings for him become all muddled? What were his thoughts on me? How could I ever repay him for his help? And what would happen when it was over?

At last Chase sighed, disrupting my inner monologue and drawing my attention back to him.

"Laurie, there's something I've been meaning to ask you," he started hesitantly. "How come a beautiful woman like you is still virgin?"

I flushed at his sudden bluntness. No one had ever asked me that, because it had never been a big deal before.

"There was never a right time."

Or a right guy.

"How come?"

I bit my suddenly parched lips, considering my words. "It's been three years since I last visited Waterfront Gardens. My life before…it was very different compared to now. I wasn't happy. I always felt something was missing. When I moved to L.A. I hoped that I could find it. So I focused on college and career, or lack thereof." I shook my head, grimacing. "All my life I had been dependent on Clint. L.A. was my first real chance to stand on my own feet and find myself. Get rid of my depression. Make something out of myself. You know, find a purpose in life."

"So you haven't dated before?"

Before?

Before now?

Before him?

Was I putting words in his mouth again?

I took my time answering his question. "I did, but…" I

looked up and drew a long breath, letting it out slowly. "It didn't go well. I didn't feel safe."

"Because you were scared of getting hurt?"

The truth was worse. So much worse. I shook my head slowly.

"No, because the last time I did, someone got killed." My breath shuddered as I remembered *his* face before he died. "I'm sorry. I don't really want to talk about it. Please don't ask."

"I would never push you." He frowned. His hand curled around mine. "Laurie, about today." His eyes locked on me gently. "I'm sorry I pushed you away. I know you wanted more, but you deserve your first time to be special. You waited so long for it to happen. I didn't want to ruin it by doing it on a backseat."

He was right, of course. A car, even one as big as the one I was sitting in, wasn't the place I'd always imagined.

But the way he said it, caring so much about it, made my body want him even more.

"So, what are you suggesting? That we go somewhere else?" I narrowed my eyes, reading between the lines.

His gaze softened. Slowly, his lips curled into the most dazzling smile, sending another wave of want through me.

Oh God.

Those dimples.

"Sometime, someplace, yes." He winked. "That is, if you

still want me to be your first." His brows shot up in mock confusion.

I blushed hard and turned my head away shyly, deliberately choosing to keep him in the dark, even though I had been so straightforward I might just as well have written 'I want you to fuck me' across my forehead.

The promise lingered in the air, so heavy I could almost touch it, and yet so far away. I wanted to come hard around his talented fingers, and yet it didn't seem like I'd ever experience any part of him inside me ever again.

He was like a dream: so real, and yet so surreal.

"I'd better go. It's getting late." I pointed at the backseat. "Have you seen my panties?"

The memory that I still had them on while getting all hot and frisky with him was vivid in my mind. After that, all became a delicious blur.

"Sure, I have."

I felt myself melting at the beautiful smile lighting up his face. For a moment, he seemed so young, so carefree; my fingers itched to pull him to me and kiss him just to see what would happen.

With a sudden move, his hand slid under the seat, and he held up my panties, dangling from his finger. I reached up to grab them, but he was faster at moving them out of my reach. "I'm keeping those as payment."

I blinked, confused. "As payment for what?"

"For making my right hand ache for a week." He stuffed them inside his pocket with a pleased expression and then turned to me again. "Ready to go home and tell Jude all our dirty secrets, or whatever you girls like doing?"

"Ha. Ha. I see your sense of humor hasn't left you. Good night, Chase." Smirking, I grabbed my bag and opened the door, but his hand curled around my upper arm, stopping me.

"That's not the only thing that hasn't left me. I still like you...a lot." Without another word, he leaned forward and gave me a short kiss on my mouth, and then whispered, "Good night, Laurie. Call me if you need anything."

I stepped out of the car, my mind spinning. He was gone the moment I reached our apartment building and had let myself inside. Hugging my body, I stood behind the glass, scanning the street, suddenly uneasy.

Even though the street was dark and deserted, I felt watched.

A shudder ran down my spine as I imagined someone lurking in the shadows, which I attributed to the fact that I didn't like to be on my own just as much as I didn't like to involve Chase in the mess that was my life. But I was doing just that. The realization that one of us would get hurt eventually sent another shiver through me.

Eventually, I headed upstairs and let myself into our apartment. The moment the door closed behind me, I exhaled a breath of relief, happy that I was back home and could finally process my thoughts.

Only eighteen days to go.

I couldn't wait to get married.

I stopped in mid-thought. That hadn't come out right. Obviously, I didn't want to get married per se. I just hoped that by marrying, everything—the threat, my fears, my questions, the constant feeling of being observed—would go away. More importantly, I had a feeling that the sole reason Chase wanted to wait was to make sure I didn't feel like I owed him for him helping me, even though he couldn't be further from the truth.

I wanted to be with him—more than anything. And not just as friends.

Sex wouldn't do it anymore.

I wanted to be more than someone he slept with.

I wanted *him*.

I wanted him to date me without all the challenges present in my life. Without being fake-married to me. Jude was right. My best friend had found a guy who wasn't just interested in helping me; he was also interested in me. Someone who might want to have a real relationship at some point. Only I wouldn't find out how real it was until this fake-marriage thing was over and we were divorced, free and ready to test how serious Chase was—a risk I was willing to take, if only to find out if his eyes were as true as his words.

If only I could control my urges around him.

Eighteen days. Of planning. Of pretending to be a loved-up couple, committed for life.

Once I reached my bedroom, I switched on the lights and closed the door. Then I threw my bag on the floor and let myself sink into my bed, ignoring the strange throbbing between my legs.

It felt strange to be back home after tonight's events—almost as if I had left a part of my old self behind with Chase. Only a few weeks ago, I didn't care much about my lack of experience when it came to sex. Maybe because I hadn't known how soft Chase's lips were or how much pleasure his presence could cause me. Now I seemed obsessed. My thoughts kept circling around him, recalling every hour we spent together, every glance he gave me, every stroke, every nuance of him, even his scent.

My heart kept wishing that it'd all work out.

All traces of my innocence were gone, replaced with longing to get to know Chase and a strong need to experience a new level of intimacy with him. He had stirred something deep inside me. It was so much more than desire or sexual longing. It was a wish to keep him long after we had signed the deal.

Only, I was too afraid of this whole marriage thing. Even though Chase wouldn't be married to me for real, he might still be feeling he had to run once things became serious.

Kicking off my shoes, I stared at the reflection in the mirror opposite my bed, wondering how I would deal with Chase's rejection once he realized just how attracted I was to him.

My phone pinged, the distracting noise echoing through the silence. I fished it out of my bag and took a deep breath before reading Chase's text.

What are you doing now? I hope you wear something short and sexy, preferably something with your sweet pussy on display.

I laughed as my fingers began to type fast.

Getting ready for sleep. And no, I wasn't planning on wearing anything. It's too hot in here.

I sat back, a grin on my face. A minute later, another message pinged back.

Damn. I wish I'd asked if you want to stay over. Can I pick you up in five min and we try again? I have a really big bed, waiting to be shared. Or so I've been told.

I stared at Chase's message. He couldn't be serious. Pick

me up at four a.m.? No chance, even though I had to admit the offer was tempting. Biting my lip, I crossed my legs under me and typed a new message.

Nice try but sorry, the ship has sailed. Remember our rules: never after midnight. And just to be clear, I expect my panties back. There's no way in hell you're keeping them.

Sleep panties! Sorry, I meant sleep tight.

A few breaths later my phone pinged again.

What panties? I think I might have lost them. No worries. I'll gladly buy you a whole drawer of them and watch you try them all on. I'll even help you pull them down.

My breath hitched as my core clenched with delicious anticipation.

Won't happen. Unless we call the whole thing off or get divorced.

Before he could continue our little game, I turned off my phone and crept under the covers with a huge smile on my face that I knew wouldn't vanish for a long time. Closing my eyes, I begged sleep to come. When it finally did, Chase's face haunted my dreams.

Chapter 8

"Wake up," Jude sang, as she knocked on my door a second before it was thrown open. "It's time to go buy a dress."

I groaned, but didn't stir in the hope she would go away. I knew she wouldn't, but at least I could pretend to not hear her. The thing with Jude was, she didn't take 'go away' for an answer; not even silence or a person's need for privacy could motivate her to back the fuck off. As if sensing my thoughts, she jumped on my bed, and began to sing the national anthem in the most cringeworthy voice one could possibly imagine, knowing all too well how much I despised noise.

Come on.

Couldn't a girl get some sleep?

Under usual circumstances, Jude had a pleasant voice. The thing was that the moment she started singing, she sounded like a cat screeching through a pipe. Jude had no talent for singing. None whatsoever. But the knowledge didn't stop her from trying at every opportunity. In fact, it had become her weapon whenever she wanted to wake me up.

"Please, shut up," I whispered, and pulled the sheets over my head again. I had managed to get all of two hours of sleep. Two hours of dreaming of Chase, his gorgeous body, my hands touching him all over, right before he was shot by an assassin and died in front of my eyes.

My subconscious was definitely trying to tell me something. I just didn't know what exactly.

Needless to say, I was tired, eager to close my eyes again and snooze through the rest of the day and get back to more pleasant dreams—anything that would remove last night's nightmare from my memory, or at least get rid of my sleep deprivation.

"Come on, Laurie. It's after lunch." Jude pulled at my sheets. "Time to buy a dress, so drag your lazy ass out of there. If you're really getting married, we better make it look damn convincing, which involves dressing the part."

I groaned and slammed a pillow over my head. "Can you give me half an hour?"

"No, make it fifteen." She yanked at the sheets, and they landed on the floor in a messy heap. "Coffee's ready. I've already called the bridal shop and made an appointment. I've heard it's the cheapest in town, and they have a sale."

Trust Jude to always find a bargain.

Who'd say no to a bargain?

Not I, and particularly not when I was strapped for cash.

"Okay." I groaned and pried one eye open, watching Jude disappear out the door.

Eighteen days to go.

With a deep breath I forced my tired body out of bed. Changing into a black shirt with jeans, I told myself that there was no need to stress out. It was just a dress. It didn't even have to be a pretty or expensive one. Only one that would do the job.

As I brushed my hair, my gaze fell on my dresser. One of the drawers was ajar. I always closed them.

Frowning, I walked closer and opened it, inspecting the personal things I kept inside. Among them was a brown wooden gift box in which I kept a necklace that once belonged to my mother. I lifted the box and opened it, my fingers itching to touch the last thing my mother wore—a reminder of her presence.

My breath hitched.

The box was empty. I rummaged through the drawer, then tossed everything onto the floor until it was empty.

There was no trace of the necklace.

"Jude!" I shouted. Her steps thudded down the hall and her head popped in an instant later.

"What? Are you done? We only have two minutes left."

"Almost." I pointed to the drawer. "Did you go through my stuff?"

Which Jude was allowed to do. She borrowed things all the time—and never forgot to give them back.

"No. Why?"

"The drawer was open. I can't find my mom's necklace." I pointed at the heap on the floor and the box. "The box is empty, and I can't find it anywhere."

"That's weird." She looked at me wide-eyed, her voice betraying her worry. "Are you sure it's gone? Maybe you just misplaced it?"

I looked around my room. Unlike Jude, I was always a bit chaotic, which was why I needed lists—a habit she had always made fun of.

"Maybe," I whispered, unconvinced.

"Let me help you," Jude offered. "We can call off the appointment and look for it. I know how important the necklace is to you, Laurie. We'll find it, you'll see."

"No, it's okay. I'll do it later when we get back. I'm sure it's somewhere here." I pointed at the mess at my feet. "Let's go."

Jude eyed me carefully. "You sure?"

I nodded with more confidence than I was feeling. There had been a time when I used to sleepwalk. The first time it happened, I was in boarding school. It had been right after I found out that my mom was sick. Sleepwalking became something of a habit that reached its peak when she died, and calmed down the moment I moved out of Waterfront Gardens. It started again five weeks ago, when nightmares plagued me.

I thought it had something to do with my nearing birthday, being faced with the reminders of my mom's suicide and my need to get those letters. Or maybe it was the result of a traumatic experience, such as being trapped in a lift with a complete stranger. Whatever caused it, one day I just woke up sprawled over the kitchen floor in front of the open fridge.

"I'm sure it's somewhere. It has to be," I said, more to convince myself than Jude. "I'm probably freaking out without reason. You know me. When I'm stressed, I tend to lose things, make a fuss, and then find them again."

"If you say so." Jude looked unconvinced but didn't comment.

Twenty minutes later, we were ready to go. During the drive I recapped to Jude last night's events, leaving out the vital details: that a man almost raped me, that Chase drove me to his special place, and that way too intimate things happened between us.

I omitted practically everything, which left Jude with the impression that Chase had picked me up, we had fast food at the drive-thru, and then he drove me home.

Nothing more. Nothing less.

There was something about Chase that I just didn't want to share every moment we spent together—maybe because I wanted to keep it all to myself until I could tell for sure where we were heading.

Of course I felt bad about keeping secrets from Jude, but I made a mental promise to tell her everything once things became less complicated.

Chapter 9

The bridal shop was tucked between a dog spa and a hairdresser's advertising quick barber's cuts for five bucks. Not exactly the type of place you'd usually expect to buy your wedding gown from, but I was strapped for cash and so, I figured, this might just be the only place where I could find something *affordable* for the 'big day,' which was what I had told Jude when she offered to play the fake bridesmaid part by helping me find the best dress I could afford for my budget.

I cringed at the word. It implied I was frugal, strapped for cash, maybe even stingy.

Budget.

I hated it almost as much as the word *poor,* because it

was associated with too many negative connotations, so I had settled for the word *affordable*.

"Are you kidding me?" Jude wrinkled her nose in obvious disgust. "Affordable is *not* the word you should be using in such a situation. It's your marriage, not dry cleaning." A few passersby turned to regard her, taking in her business suit and stilettos, the oversized sunglasses perched on her head, and the designer scarf tied around her flawless neck. My old business suit fitted her like a sheath, hugging her curves in all the right places and riding up her long legs. Needless to say, it suited her way better than it did me. She looked like a high-flying Californian lawyer that would soon be featured in *Forbes,* while I usually looked like a frumpy mess. Add that knowledge to the fact that I was about to get married to Chase in cheap polyester and I could already see a huge cloud of depression hovering over my head.

"How has your week been at work?" I asked, eager to draw the attention back to her. No matter how late Jude had arrived home the night before and how many margaritas she had downed, knowing her, she probably had gotten up at five as usual to check on her blog and entertain the gazillions of Facebook fans she had accumulated.

"You know me. I can't talk about it." She waved her hand.

She was being superstitious, as usual, and she wasn't

going to talk about it so she wouldn't jinx it.

"Got it," I said, pushing the door to the bridal shop open.

A bell above the door chimed in a pleasant tinkling sound.

"I'm Casey. Can I help you?" A shop assistant in her mid- to late twenties ambled over, a bored expression on her face.

"She's getting married," Jude said, pointing at me.

Casey's gaze snapped in my direction and her eyes narrowed on me, probably taking my measurements already. "We cater to every bride's need. When's the big day?"

"In two, three weeks max," I said, and almost toppled over from embarrassment as I caught the knowing expression in her eyes. Her gaze traveled down my abdomen, then back up to my face.

"I'm not pregnant," I hurried to add.

Casey inclined her head and smiled sweetly, probably not believing a word I had said. After all, wasn't an unexpected pregnancy the main reason why most people got married nowadays?

"They only met, like, a week ago," Jude said, not really helping. "Literally."

I shot her an irritated look but she just shrugged.

"Great," Casey said, a little bit too excited. "We won't have to worry about a bloated abdomen, then. Did you have anything in mind? Maybe a silhouette you've been dreaming of since you were a girl? Here at Wedding Bells I'm sure you'll find the right dress."

I shook my head, slightly intimidated by the sudden knowledge that choosing a gown was yet another step toward this marriage. Soon there would be no turning back.

Run, Hanson.

But instead of following my brain's extremely wise command, I stood rooted to the spot, frozen in time and space, unable to utter a single word.

"She's never been the marrying kind, you know." Jude laughed. "It sort of jumped into her lap."

"Okay," Casey said, drawing out a paper pad. "In that case, I'll ask you a couple of questions to determine what you're looking for as we go along. Sound good?"

"Absolutely," Jude exclaimed for me.

Wow, she really *did* want me to go through with it.

No pressure, at all.

"Can you please follow me to the showroom?" Casey ushered us along, her voice oozing pride. "You'll find we store almost all brands in all sizes for each and everyone."

We followed her through the showroom to the back, where the shop seemed to extend into a warehouse. I had never seen so many clothes. Rows and rows of white and cream fabric seemed to stretch on forever. To my right was a selection of gowns in colors raging from pastels to bold red and black. Some were short; others cascaded onto the floor in a multitude of ruffles. All I could do was stare—and not out of excitement. I was completely and utterly overwhelmed. I never thought a wedding dress would come in so many variations.

Where the heck would I even begin?

"Not bad," Jude said, nodding appreciatively. "We should be done in half an hour. An hour tops."

Casey smiled politely. "Let's get started, then." She opened her notebook and looked up at me. "Do you want short or long?"

"Ah—" I opened my mouth to speak, but Jude cut me off.

"I was thinking long. But—" She drew a sharp breath and let it out in a loud huff. "She has nice legs and it would be a shame if she didn't show them, so short would work for us, too."

Casey jotted down every word. "Long but we're not ruling out short."

"Exactly." I nodded.

"Okay." Casey peered around the warehouse and then began to move racks around, all the while asking more questions. "What about the color? Do you want to go with traditional white? Off-white? Cream? Or something bolder? Some brides like red for good luck."

I hesitated as I tried to imagine myself in a wedding

gown. White always washed me out. Anything pastel only managed to emphasize the tiny freckles on my face. But I couldn't possibly go with a bright color. Not if I wanted Clint and everyone else to buy my bluff.

"We like white," Jude said. "And off-white." She held a piece of fabric up to my face and squinted. "Cream, too."

"So, nothing too bold." Casey scribbled furiously, her gaze focused on the notepad.

"Actually—"

I cut Jude off. "No. It has to look like a real wedding. I need to have a traditional white dress."

Casey looked up sharply, and for a moment I thought I saw suspicion in her eyes. Jude let out a shrill laugh.

"You just made it sound like you're only marrying to get a visa," Jude said, patting my back with a hint of nervousness. "You're hilarious."

Oh my God. I could have killed her. Casey's gaze darted toward the door, and for a second I thought she might just dash out and call the immigration office. Trust Jude to say something that might just get me arrested.

"Funny." I smirked. "Can we finish, please? What other questions do you have for me?"

"Sleeves, cut?" Casey said after a long, hesitant pause.

No idea.

I looked at Jude for help, but she kept her mouth shut.

"Well, I think I'll go with sleeves," I said. "Long sleeves

made of chiffon or organza."

"Bad idea, Laurie. It's too hot. Better go with short," Jude cut in, turning to Casey as she smiled and stepped forward, ready to take over again. "She has a problem with her upper arms, so, naturally, she tries to hide them with sleeves. But straps would look good on her, too. Maybe even backless. Or halter top." She eyed me up and down. Her eyes narrowed knowingly, then she scanned the racks.

"Something sexy that isn't too old-fashioned. Something like…" Frowning in concentration, Jude began sifting through the racks furiously, pulling at the plastic covering most of the dresses. "Empire waist to emphasize her cleavage. Or a corset."

As Jude continued her chatter, Casey's pen flew over the paper effortlessly. At some point I tuned out, realizing Casey had stopped writing and was just nodding politely, wide-eyed. Eventually, Jude stopped and Casey asked us to wait in the showroom while she put together a possible selection of gowns that I might like.

To be honest, I was surprised Casey had not thrown us out yet, what with Jude's pointing at countless dresses and not able to make up her mind on what we really wanted.

"This is exciting and so much fun," Jude said as we took our seats patiently.

I wasn't convinced, not least because my head was throbbing and I couldn't picture myself dressed in a wedding gown, let alone walking down the aisle. It all seemed like a surreal dream—pleasant, but a dream nonetheless. However, I was thankful for Jude's help, so I smiled and watched her type on her smartphone, probably tweeting to the whole world about her experience.

At least twenty minutes passed before Casey returned pushing in a rack with gowns, and then another, and one more—all based on the questionnaire she had filled out for me.

"Didn't she say she was going to pick just a *few* dresses for you? I guess someone's having a tough time making decisions," Jude whispered to me, and stashed her phone back inside her handbag, ready to give the dress her entire attention.

"Well, since you couldn't really give me *any* pointers," Casey said, shooting me an exasperated look, "I had to choose something from everything."

"That's not true," Jude said defiantly. "We know exactly what we're looking for, don't we, Laurie? And we're in a hurry, so if we can't find anything here, we'll have to look elsewhere. And that would be such a shame, because…" She left the rest hanging in the air. Poor Casey's face turned ashen. I could almost see her thoughts written across her forehead. Trying to find the right dress for me, she'd messed up the entire warehouse and now she feared we'd leave without purchasing anything.

"All right," Casey said, pointing to a rack. "This one caught your attention right from the beginning." She gave Jude an exasperated look as she pointed to the other racks. "The rest is supposed to match your questionnaire. I suggest you go through them, and pick out what you like so we can narrow your choice down a bit."

"These look great. Thank you," I said, scanning the selection of gowns, and stood to inspect them closer. My fingers brushed over chiffon sheaths and countless yards of tulle, and settled on a cream silk dress with a ribboned embroidered bodice. No tulle. No ruffles. No trail. Just a pure, clean silhouette that I could wear anywhere, which, for some reason, mattered.

"It's beautiful." I nodded slowly, astonished by how soft the fabric was.

"Good choice, Laurie. It's absolutely stunning," Jude whispered behind me. "You should try it on."

While she took a seat outside the fitting room, sipping the glass of champagne Casey had offered her, I slipped on the dress. The moment I stepped outside, I could her Jude swallow down a huge gulp of champagne, and for a moment I feared the worst.

"What?" I asked anxiously, my hands brushing nervously over the silky fabric. Both Jude and Casey had become quiet as they stared at me. After what seemed like an eternity, Jude stood and inched closer, pressing her hand against her chest.

"You have to have it, Laurie," she whispered. "It's perfect."

I knew that tone and the slight tremor in her voice. She was mesmerized, just like I was. Completely sold. And she wouldn't stop talking about it until one of us purchased it.

Chapter 10

"It really is," I agreed. Even though I wasn't exactly an expert in fashion, I could tell this was no ordinary dress. I had never seen such extravagance in something so simple. I could already see myself in it, walking down the aisle with Chase waiting at the altar, giving me the 'wow' look and then kissing me in that dress.

Holy cow!

Where did that come from? For a bride who didn't want to get married, I was getting way too much into this. But I didn't mind. This dress would be mine for one day and I'd feel amazing in it. It might not be the wedding of a lifetime, but it would be my first wedding, and while fake, it would be with the first man who proposed such a sordid idea to me.

"When people fall in love at first sight with a dress, it's usually meant for them," Jude said in delight when I returned, the dress wrapped over my arm. "It's absolutely perfect, Laurie. You have to buy it."

"Okay. I'll take it."

"I agree. It's perfect for you," Casey chimed in, reaching for it. "Don't wait, or you'll regret it. You'll look like a million dollars."

From all the things she could have said, this was the most clichéd…but I didn't mind. The dress was beautiful, and I had no doubt it would look amazing on any woman of any shape and on any day of any season. I reached for the cream material, marveling again at how soft it felt between my fingers, and then the tag caught my eye.

"Vera Wang?" Jude and I exclaimed in unison.

Of course it had to be by one of the most expensive fashion designers in the world.

My mouth dropped open as I glimpsed the price, and for a moment I thought it might be a joke, because no dress could possibly be so expensive. Silence ensued in the room as a lump suddenly rose in my throat. For a few moments I could barely breathe.

The gorgeous dress would never be mine. Not in a million years, because I couldn't afford it. Chase would never see how good it fitted me.

I stared at the dress until Jude's words pulled me out of my mounting depression.

"I thought it was a bargain shop," Jude said half accusingly, turning to Casey, her face a reproachful mask, as if she was to blame.

I peered at Casey, who stood rooted to the spot, a tight smile on her lips.

"It is." She nodded slowly. "It's fifty per cent off. We could even arrange a loan for you." Her expression was unperturbed, as though she had experienced such a reaction before. Given the price tag, no surprise there.

Her gaze traveled from Jude and settled on me questioningly, as she waited for my answer. Did she really think that women who couldn't afford such luxury would take out a loan to get it?

Probably—if it were a real wedding.

For a moment I felt almost tempted to do the same.

But it wasn't a real wedding in my case. I had to keep that tiny detail in mind.

"I cannot afford it," I said. "Do you have something more affordable?"

Oh, how I hated the word.

"You heard the bride-to-be. We cannot afford it," Jude said. She sounded so stressed out that I turned to her.

"It's just a dress, Jude. I'm sure there are others that will fit me just as well," I remarked weakly, even though I knew nothing I could possibly say would make Jude feel better. When she knew there was something I liked, she *had* to have it for me. There simply was no other way.

"But you said it's the perfect dress," Jude whispered, and turned to Casey with a scowl, grabbing the dress as if it was the holy grail of marriages or the only path to redemption. "We need to have it. Give me solutions. Give me something I can work with. Maybe another fifty per cent discount?" She laughed, even though I could hear the gravity in her voice.

"Maybe your parents or the groom's parents would like to pay," Casey suggested, oblivious to Jude's pleading glance.

I shook my head and shot her a warning glance. There was no point in getting upset over a dress, was there? And yet Jude's eyes darted across the shiny floor as her mind searched for possibilities. I had no doubt she'd soon come up with some absurd idea. I could even imagine her just grabbing the dress and simply walking out of the shop without paying.

I laughed inwardly. It was the last thing I needed.

"Can we maybe rent it?" Jude persisted. "I mean, it would be just for one day."

Casey smiled apologetically. "I'm sorry. We can't because it's a designer dress. That would break our company policy, but we have other, cheaper gowns, which might be to your liking. We have imports from China, which unfortunately all come in one size fits all, but that doesn't mean you won't look gorgeous in one of them."

"What crappy policy is that?" Jude asked. "You should offer the option of borrowing. People with little money should be able to wear designer clothes."

"It's not that kind of shop," Casey said, keeping her cool.

Jude scowled and opened her mouth, then shut it again.

I pulled at her arm. If I didn't manage to stop Jude anytime soon, Casey might just throw us out. I figured the faster we got out of here, the better. Because soon I'd have to pry Jude off this dress with a screwdriver.

"We'll think about it. Thanks." I yanked at Jude's arm again, without much success, then tried to force the dress out of her hand, but Jude's grip remained surprisingly firm.

"You could charge it to your credit card," Jude said, turning to me, desperate for any solution.

"It's maxed out, Jude." I must have mentioned that countless times, together with the fact that I could barely make my minimum repayments, and yet she still grimaced.

"So is mine this month. Dammit." She tapped her fingers against her lips in thought. "Let's charge an entrance fee, then. Everyone who wants to attend the wedding ceremony is required to make a down payment toward the dress."

Not bad, only… "There isn't going to be a ceremony because we're eloping."

My remark managed to silence her for all of three seconds, during which her brain never stopped working. I could tell from her expression that she thought she had found the solution to my problem a moment before she opened her mouth to speak, her eyes twinkling. "Chase is an actor. I'm sure he'll want his bride to look good in the wedding album, particularly if we're to sell the wedding photos to the paparazzi."

I almost threw my hands up in exasperation. "It's not a real wedding, Jude. We don't love each other. Heck, he couldn't care less about me, so trust me when I say a.) there won't be a wedding album, and b.) Chase will probably want to get it over and done with without spending any of his money, and c.) you're being creepy as hell. He'll run for the hills the moment he hears I'm all serious about this wedding. Honestly, Jude, have you ever heard about a guy who cares about dresses, unless he's very much into fashion?" I raised my brows meaningfully.

Jude crossed her arms over her chest with a stubborn expression on her face. "You're not even going to ask him? He might think differently, if only he saw the dress."

Oh God.

Would Jude ever give up? I doubted it.

I took a deep, calming breath and let it out slowly. "No,

I'm not going to ask him. Now, please be reasonable. It's just a dress. It's not even the prettiest gown in store."

Which was a big, fat lie.

It was the most stunning dress I had ever laid my eyes on.

"If we look around, I'm sure we'll find something cheaper and more flattering."

"No. You don't understand, Laurie. This is the dress you fell in love with at first sight. It's a good-luck dress."

Oh, shoot! She was going all spiritual on me.

I followed the swooping motion of her arms. "Just admit, it beats the others by a mile. And you'll be so pretty. Think how glowing you'll look. The dress will practically do the job of getting married for you. Imagine all the stress going away, the moment you just say yes in this dress."

I sank onto the couch and let out an exasperated sigh.

This would take time.

I always knew that Jude could sell anything to anyone. I just never expected her to be as pushy as a car insurance salesman, insisting you buy something that was a worse investment than the state lottery.

Shaking my head, I listened to Jude counting all the reasons why I just *had* to get the dress.

It wasn't just a dress for Jude simply because, unlike me, she was very much into fashion. She wanted me to look good, and I couldn't blame her, only I wasn't going to pay thousands of dollars on a piece of exquisite fabric—no matter how flattering it might be.

We stared each other down in angry silence until Casey disrupted our glares with a simple cough to announce her presence.

"I understand your problem," Casey said slowly. "I think I can help."

"Oh? You can help?" Jude's head snapped in her direction immediately. "We want to hear it."

I rolled my eyes. Nope, I wasn't going to get a store card, even if it promised a repayment-free period, or whatever other strategies stores came up with to fool female shopaholics like Jude to part with their money.

"Follow me," Casey said conspiratorially. She locked the store and led us through the warehouse into the backyard that led to a parking lot. I wanted to ask where we were going, but Jude shushed me with a single determined look.

We crossed the parking lot and entered a run-down building on the other side of the road, then climbed up the staircase. Casey unlocked a door on the second floor and ushered us into a narrow hall with countless pictures on the walls.

It was someone's apartment, no doubt about that. I suspected Casey's, until a female voice called out her name.

"Nana?" Casey said, gesturing us to follow her into a surprisingly spacious living room with yet more picture frames arranged across the old furniture—many of which showed children's faces and a large family sitting together.

"You bringing over friends?" The old woman was sitting on the couch. With her keen eyes resting on us, she put down her embroidery and stood, inching closer. Her warm gaze brushed us and settled on me.

"This is my grandma. She's a seamstress," Casey explained by means of introduction. "I think she can help. It might not be a Vera Wang dress, but she can create a very similar style of dress in a very similar material for the fraction of a price. And between you and me"—she winked mischievously—"Grandma could give Vera a run for her money. But that's just my opinion."

***

"She's all about love at first sight," Casey explained as she invited us to sit at the round table. "My grandparents were married for fifty-eight years. Right, Nana?"

The old woman nodded, a kind expression on her face as her eyes lit up with fond memories. "We got engaged and married within a year of meeting. It was love at first sight. The first time I met Graham, he told me that I was worth waiting for. And I thought that was the kind of the person I could imagine my life with. We were poor, but we had a full life. We did everything together. It was the secret of our relationship. Sticking together. Sharing our passions."

"Wow," I whispered, impressed. "Fifty-eight years. That's a long time."

Nana had insisted we had some iced tea before she took my measurements, so I sipped on my glass and listened, enjoying the old woman's stories. After all, she was someone who knew how to make a relationship work.

"Not long enough." She smiled gently, and for a second I could feel her pain. As much as I wanted to ask what happened to Graham, I just couldn't, because I knew he would never have left her of his own free will. The greatest love stories always encountered the greatest loss. I couldn't imagine loving so deeply and losing it all in the blink of an eye.

Nana misinterpreted my smile for an invitation to continue. "My mother always told me that the moment the right man enters your life, all hell breaks loose. She couldn't be more right. Suddenly you have needs you never knew existed, and those urges can only be stilled by him because he's everywhere. In your mind. In your heart." Pausing, she pointed at her chest. "And surely in your panties. I used to laugh, until I met Graham. Everything clicked from day one, and I just couldn't say no."

"That's amazing," I said, genuinely impressed, my mind replaying her words. Fifty-eight years was a long time. I had never been that committed to anything. Not even to a single haircut. I sure couldn't see myself hanging on to a man for such a long time.

"Best decision of my life. Trust me, the right man will sneak into your heart before you know it and then there's no going back. There is no mistaking love. That's why marriage is such a beautiful thing that doesn't need to wait." She eyed me full of curiosity, crossing her hands, now old with age, on the table. Her wedding ring sparkled, as though beckoning to me, urging me to believe in the kind of love I was so afraid to peer at.

No more running. Time to believe in it all.

In a world where over billions of people existed, there had to be someone for me. Someone who might stir certain feelings, just like Chase did. Someone who might look as good as him.

I stopped in my thoughts. Obviously, that someone wasn't Chase.

I liked him, but not like that. Or did I?

Even though he had asked me to marry him, it was hardly the same thing.

"So, my niece tells me you met the love of your life just days ago and now you want to get married." Nana shot me a knowing look. "I understand you're strapped for cash and in dire need of a dress."

"Yes, this one." Jude held up the Vera Wang dress that was still draped over her arm. She hadn't let it out of her sight. "But we cannot afford it."

Nana nodded, her wrinkled skin crinkling at the corners of her eyes.

"You're lucky. I've been a dressmaker for years. I'd be happy to help to sew your wedding gown. May I?" She reached out for the dress and then inspected the inseams before looking up. "I can do something like this."

"Thank you," I said, feeling utter gratitude. While she continued to chatter with Jude, I asked for the restroom, the woman's words still ringing in my ears. Obviously, I couldn't care less about instant attraction, but in a twisted way, her words made perfect sense.

Someday I'd find someone worthy of my heart, but that moment hadn't come. My heart would stay out of my marriage to Chase.

This was the opportunity I had been waiting for, and now it was time to commit to my decision of doing everything possible to uncover the credibility of my mother's last words to me.

Returning to our table, I expected Jude to be immersed in deep and meaningful conversation, but to my surprise she had already paid an advance for the dress, and Casey and she were now waiting for me.

All I could do was nod as I was asked to strip down to my underwear, and Casey's grandmother began to take my measurements while Jude and Casey haggled over a price for yet another dress Jude insisted she needed for herself as the bridesmaid. Trust Jude to use the opportunity to get a dress she had always dreamed of custom designed. I knew she was going to use her gown as a cocktail dress with that extra zing.

Thirty minutes later, Casey accompanied us out with the promise my dress would be ready within five days. We exchanged phone numbers in case one of us had questions, and then Jude left for the studio.

As I made my way back home I felt flushed with both excitement and dread.

I was going to wear a knockoff dress.

Given that Chase and I were marriage shams, how fitting!

For the umpteenth time, I wondered how I got myself into this situation. Under any other circumstances I would have run rather than let Jude make all the decisions, but those weren't normal circumstances. I needed a dress that would fool everyone into thinking the wedding was real. And then there was the excitement. I was getting married. And even though everything was fake, I hoped the dress would be stunning and I'd look beautiful for Chase.

Chapter 11

Our apartment was situated in a converted warehouse that had been remodeled into affordable two-bedroom apartments. Ours was the one on the first floor. By the time I reached it, my back was slick with sweat and my clothes had become two sizes too small, sticking to my skin. I had barely unlocked the door when my cell rang.

The caller id showed an unknown number.

I slammed the door shut behind me and slumped to the floor, suddenly exhausted and flushed from the heat outside.

"Can we talk?" It was Chase, and judging by the urgency in his voice he wasn't calling to enquire about the progress of our wedding preparations.

I frowned. Alarm bells started to ring in my head. It wasn't like Chase to be formal. His tone ominous. Even though we'd had a good time the day before, I couldn't stop the nervous flip my stomach did.

Something was wrong.

Or why else would he want to talk?

"Sure." I hesitated. "What about?"

"Great. I'm just around the corner. I'll be over in five."

And then he hung up, ignoring my question. I stared at the phone, flummoxed. What the hell was that all about? And how could he possibly be over in five minutes? Unless…

He was around the corner, literally, because an instant later the intercom rang.

Shit!

I peered around, panicky, suddenly aware of the fact that I was a sweaty mess, and in desperate need of a shower. And not only that; the apartment didn't look much better. I jumped up and began to strip off my clothes while simultaneously picking up Jude's scattered interior design magazines and clothes. I had barely made it to the bathroom to discard my armful of clothes and magazines when the doorbell rang.

Someone must have buzzed him in, because he was here. Right behind the door, inches separating us.

I stood frozen to the spot, unsure whether to claim I

wasn't at home after all, or open the door, but pretend that I was too busy to let him in.

The doorbell rang again, the piercing sound lingering in the air. An instant later, Chase's faint voice echoed over.

"Laurie? I know you're in there. Open up."

Was he angry? I had no idea, but I didn't like the sense of urgency and seriousness in his voice. He rapped at the door. Once. Twice. With a sigh, I shrugged into a bathrobe and wrapped the cord tightly around my waist, then pulled my hair up in a ponytail. As soon as I opened the door, Chase barged in, hot waves of anger wafting from him.

"Hello to you, too," I muttered, closing the door behind him.

Ignoring me, he headed straight for the living room and slumped down on the sofa, then turned to face me, eyes blazing, his beautiful lips pressed in a tight line.

What the heck did I do wrong?

"Are you okay?" I asked, sliding down opposite him with as much distance as was possible between us. "You seem a bit upset." Upset was an understatement. He seemed livid.

"Are you alone?" His voice was hard as his eyes scanned the room in search for Jude.

I nodded and he breathed out, but his muscles remained unnaturally tense. "We don't have much time."

I regarded him, confused. "For what?"

"You went to choose a wedding dress," he said reproachfully, ignoring me again.

I nodded slowly. "Yes, Chase. I did."

"Why?"

His question caught me off guard.

"Why?" I laughed. Had he smashed in his head or something? "In case you have forgotten, we're supposed to get married. I need to make it look authentic." A wave of shame washed over me at the cold look in his eyes. He thought me desperate. Or maybe realization had dawned on him and now he was having cold feet at the prospect of tying the knot with a complete stranger who might decide to file for spousal support, or worse—half of his belongings. Given that he seemed to own more than I did, I wouldn't have been surprised if the latter was the case.

Suddenly, my air supply was cut off and I felt as though the ceiling was about to crash down on me.

What was I doing, pulling him into this mess with me? How the hell could I have relied on him to follow through with the marriage?

I walked to the window and opened it to let in the warm afternoon air, then turned around, watching him closely.

"What's going on, Chase?" I asked.

"Let me rephrase," Chase said, his voice low but cold as ice. "One moment you don't want this, and the next you buy a dress. You haven't thought this through, Laurie."

"Believe me, I have," I muttered. For years I had been planning on getting those letters in the hope that it would give me the chance to look into the mystery that had consumed most of my life.

"No, you don't understand." Chase let out a slow breath. "I mean you sent me a text talking about calling the whole thing off. Are you sure you want to go through with this? Because you seem to constantly change your mind, and I have no time for this. I have no time for playing games."

"Yes, I'm sure."

He looked so unconvinced, my heart dropped. Or maybe it wasn't conviction, but disappointment with my answer. Maybe he hoped I'd say that we were making a mistake.

There was my answer.

I crossed my arms over my chest and regarded him coldly, waiting for him to take the first step.

"What?"

"Nothing." I shook my head slowly. "Look, if you don't want to do this, it's fine. You don't even need to tell me. Just get up and leave, and I'll get the message. There won't be any hard feelings."

His hard expression softened a little. "I never said that."

"What are you trying to say, then, because I sure as hell don't understand you. Do you want out? Is that why you're here?"

"I—" His words failed him. I could see it from the various expressions crossing his face. Something bothered him. Something he didn't want to share with me. I hadn't known Chase for long, but for some reason I could sense that he was torn—confused, even.

For a moment, silence ensued between us. I bit my lip hard until it burst between my teeth. My tongue flicked over a drop of blood inside my mouth.

"How did you even know I went shopping?" I avoided the word 'dress' on purpose. Chase shook his head grimly, but remained silent.

There was only one possibility.

"Jude told you," I said. It wasn't a question; it was a statement. "Either that, or you followed us."

Chase looked up and our gazes met, and for a moment something shimmered in his eyes. "I didn't follow you."

The dull pain in my head roared to a full throbbing pulsation. So she had told him.

I didn't like the fact that my best friend was telling him things behind my back. Maybe she was way more smitten with him than I had realized. Or maybe she hadn't dropped the idea of asking him to help with the wedding costs. Either way, I didn't like it.

How dare she not tell me?

"She shouldn't have talked to you," I said.

"She wouldn't have if I hadn't called her."

A pang of jealousy hit me in the pit of my stomach. "Why did you?" I asked, even though it was none of my business. I didn't own him. We weren't even in a relationship. His silence worried me. Suddenly I could imagine Chase smiling at Jude with the same passion he had invested in my smile, asking her on a date, or sending her flirty messages.

"Chase?" My voice sounded choked. "Why *did* you call her?"

"Because I wanted to surprise you."

My heart began to pound harder as I leaned back in shock, then surprise. A minute passed in silence, followed by another.

"With what?" I narrowed my eyes, not trusting him.

His lips twitched at the corners, and for the first time his anger seemed lifted, giving him the carefree expression I had glimpsed before. And then it disappeared again and a frown took its place. "Doesn't matter now." Sitting back, he ran a hand through his disheveled hair, hesitating again.

He still hadn't answered my question why he was here. The realization bothered me.

"Just so that you know, Chase. You don't need to go through with it, you know. I promise you I'll understand if you want out."

For a moment his expression brightened and I thought I

saw relief in his eyes. He wanted out. The realization hurt me more than I cared to admit. I smiled bitterly as I realized just how much I had wanted to go through with it all. Was it so bad that I had been looking forward to marrying him, even though it was all fake, arranged to suit a purpose?

Stupid. Stupid. Stupid.

How could I have been so stupid and let my guard down like that when it wasn't even real? I should have trusted my feelings. I shouldn't have believed it was too good to be true. Too easy. I should never have gone shopping for a dress. So many should and should-nots, but the knowledge didn't ease my anger.

Interpreting his silence as agreement, I nodded.

"All right." I sighed. "Then let's call it all off," I whispered. "You can leave now."

"Laurie?" He hesitated, looking for words, and then his cell phone rang. Chase pulled it out of his pocket and peered at the caller ID, his frown instantly deepening. For a second, he just stared at it with the kind of mistrust reserved for an attacking cobra. The ringing stopped, only to resume again. And still he seemed to harbor no intentions of wanting to answer.

"You should take it," I said nonchalantly. "It might be important, you know." *Like a secret girlfriend*, I added mentally, realizing just how bitter I sounded. He could have as many dates as he wanted. It was none of my concern.

For all I cared, he could date Jude. Actually, that one might hurt like hell, but there was nothing I could do about it.

At least I hadn't slept with him. It would just have been a mistake; it would have left my heart scarred.

The phone kept ringing.

"It's not important," Chase said, still staring at the screen.

"How do you know? It might be." Why the heck did I keep insisting? Because I wanted a sign—any sign—that would shatter my stupid hopes. The kind of hopes I should never have allowed myself to have. When did that even happen?

Chase hesitated. I knew he had made a decision when his shoulders slumped and he lifted the phone to his ear, pressing the green button in the process. He didn't say a word, just listened to the other end of the line. The words were too muffled to understand, but I could tell from Chase's angry expression that he didn't like whatever was being said. And then he muttered, "Okay. Got it," and hung up.

That was it?

I frowned. Chase was a professional actor. I could only guess that whoever had been on the other end of the line had some sort of authority, like his agent or manager. Was it possible that his agent had found out Chase was going to get married and told him it was a bad move that could possible destroy his career?

Possible. I wouldn't have been surprised if that was the problem.

Regarding him, I bit my lip again so I wouldn't ask the countless questions burning on my lips. Chase's eyes refocused on me, his blue gaze as deep as an ocean on a winter's night, and just as troubled.

"You should have asked me about the dress," he began. "I would have come with you to help you choose it."

Huh?

I blinked in disbelief, unsure if I should be frank or play confused. I decided directness was the better way to get answers.

"Is that why you're so angry? That you didn't get your say in the matter?" I raised my brows. Was he turning out to be a controlling nutcase? Did he have a problem with a woman taking charge of a situation?

"No. That's not it." He shook his head slowly, his eyes still ablaze with a spark of irritation I couldn't place. Whatever battle he was fighting, he obviously preferred to keep it to himself.

"What's going on?" I threw my hands up in exasperation. "Please help me understand, because I'm losing my wits with you."

Finally his expression relaxed and he leaned back against the cushions.

"Look." He drew a sharp breath and looked up. "I just wanted to surprise you with a dress, because I thought you would forget."

"Oh."

Had I been misinterpreting his behavior?

"But it's okay. You've obviously made up your mind, so…" He shrugged, and a hint of a smile appeared on his lips, veiling whatever was going on inside him. "Anyway, I've instructed a friend of mine to get the necessary paperwork done by the weekend. If you don't mind." He raised a brow. And just like, that his mood lifted.

I swallowed hard as my heartbeat picked up in speed. He had what?

No going back.

Did I even *want* to go back? My mind was spinning, frozen from the hundreds of swirling thoughts racing through it, but even worse was my heart and its hopeful fluttering.

"Are you sure?" I asked, plopping down next to him, unable to stop the renewed hope rising within me—stronger than before.

"Of course I'm sure. Once everything's sorted, we're ready to go." He paused as he leaned forward. "There's just one problem, Laurie. You might not like it."

I grimaced. "What it is?"

"I've just landed a job, which requires me to travel to

NYC. I tried to change the time, but they didn't agree, so…" He shrugged, his eyes boring into me. "We'll have to get married sooner. Like next Tuesday. Will that be a problem?"

My eyes widened at the word 'sooner.'

"Next Tuesday?" I swallowed hard.

Holy cow!

That soon?

He nodded slowly.

I had it all wrong. Chase had been serious. He was really doing it. As if confirming my thoughts, he continued, "There won't be time to send out invitations. No time to invite your family or friends." He sounded apologetic, as if not having a huge party was indeed a problem.

"Your birthday might be in three weeks, but with me gone, this is the only time I can offer you, so…" He shrugged, leaving the rest unspoken. He didn't need to spell out the obvious. I had to be married by my birthday, which left us to do the deed when it was convenient for him, which was fine by me. "So…what do you think?"

"I think it's…great." In spite of my nerves, I smiled. "Let's do it on Tuesday, then. Sounds as good as any other day."

His brows shot up. "What about your family and friends?"

"It's just a fake marriage, Chase. Besides, I don't really

have a family. My grandparents died a few years ago after my mom's death. So, it's just me and you and Jude."

"All right. That's settled, then." He smiled, all traces of anger gone. "Do you have any special plans? I was going to invite you over for dinner so we could talk." His lips twitched at the corners again. For a moment I just stared at him, astounded both by how quickly he could change his mood, and by the fact that he looked so damn sexy doing it.

Focus, Hanson!

He still wanted to talk. What else did he want to talk about? Because there sure was nothing to discuss. Sign the papers and then move on. But instead of asking the obvious, I found myself simply nodding and mumbling, "Okay."

"Tonight?"

"I can do that." My heart beat so fast, I feared it might just burst out of my chest. He looked at his watch and stood, signaling the end of our conversation. "About seven?"

"Sounds great."

"I'll pick you up."

"Thanks." I tried to sound nonchalant, but failed miserably. Chase headed for the door and I followed a step behind. When he stopped mid-stride, I bumped into him. His arm went around my waist to steady me, but instead my bathrobe almost came undone. My hands clenched quickly at the fabric, pressing it against my chest, while my eyes remained connected with Chase's. There was something in his gaze—dark and broody, and much too disconcerting.

I groaned inwardly at the way my insides seemed to melt, giving way to a deliciously warm sensation I had never felt for another man.

Chase lowered his head and for a moment I held my breath, both hoping and fearing that he might be about to kiss me. To my dismay, he stopped an inch from my lips, and when he spoke his hot breath caressed my skin.

"You need to learn to fall with no safety cushion, Laurie."

"Why would I want that?" I whispered, unable to control the shaking of my voice.

"Because I'm right there to catch you. No matter what happens. Just don't play with me."

No matter what happens.

Dangerous words coming from a man like him. I swallowed past the sudden lump in my throat as my heart did a flip-flop. Chase smiled, and in that instant I forgot the world around me. I forgot that we were two strangers soon to be married for convenience. I forgot that I wasn't supposed to open up to him, because I couldn't lose my heart to a man.

Lifting on my toes, I raised my mouth to his until our lips connected in a brief but tender kiss. And then I pulled back.

"See you later," I said.

"You can't be serious." Chase groaned but didn't make any attempt at trying to get more than I was ready to give.

"What? I was just trying to say thank you." I squealed as his hand palmed the nape of my neck and his fingers curled in my hair, pulling slightly but not enough to hurt.

"Watching you in that bathrobe and imagining you naked underneath it was hard enough," he said hoarsely. "Now you're seeing me off with a sweet kiss and expect me to leave unaffected?"

Holy cow!

He was affected?

I could barely contain my stupid grin.

"How about you give me a little more?" Chase asked.

My core began to pulse at the insinuation in his deep voice, and a warm sensation pooled between my legs. As though he sensed my sudden arousal, his hand moved between the layers of my bathrobe to stroke my abdomen, inches from the hidden spot that no man had ever touched—except him. And it was such a good memory. One I ached to repeat. But if I didn't resist now, I might just find myself entangled in the sheets with Chase on top of me. The thought wasn't half bad, only Jude would be back soon. How could I possibly explain that to her?

"No. Not now." I pushed his hand away, gently but

determinedly, even though my whole body screamed for him, begging my brain to let it happen.

"Why not?" Chase whispered against my skin, his hot breath caressing my earlobe.

So close. Too close.

I shook my head, suddenly trembling, and not from the cold. "I'm sorry. I can't. I—" I moistened my lips and forced myself to meet his heated gaze. It was so obvious what he wanted, but I couldn't give it to him now. Even though I wanted to. Madly. In fact, it was the one thing I could think about before falling asleep. "If we want our arrangement to work, we can't get involved like *this*." I pointed at the air between us in the hope he wouldn't expect me to spell out the obvious, because I knew if he kept talking about it I might just change my mind.

"Maybe. For the time being." Chase grimaced and pulled back but didn't let go of me immediately.

I set my jaw. "What the hell's that supposed to mean?"

"We need to set some ground rules before I lose control and can't be held accountable for my actions," Chase said, grinning. "In fact, I think I've just come up with the perfect plan. Dinner. Seven sharp. And don't be late."

And with that he turned around and left, slamming the door behind him, leaving me standing with my arms wrapped around myself and absolutely no idea what the hell he had been talking about.

Chapter 12

What the hell just happened? That was the one question that lingered in my mind for the next three hours.

Blowing hot and cold.

That's what Chase was. Erratic and impulsive—a dangerous combination in a man. I realized that ever since meeting him, I had tried my damnedest to place him…without much success, and for the first time I asked myself whether our marriage, as short as it would be until we got divorced, would be as unpredictable as the man himself.

Staring at my reflection in the mirror, I smoothed my hands down my buttoned blouse and pencil skirt, and then took a deep breath, readying myself for the evening ahead when I heard the door.

"How was it?" I asked as soon as Jude let herself in.

She dropped her handbag on the floor and took her time slipping out of her shoes, all the while avoiding my gaze.

I regarded her intently as I tried to read her expression. Was her silence a good or a bad thing? I had no clue, and had almost assumed the worst when a smile lit up her face. "They want me back."

I drew her into a hug, proud of her.

"I told you. Didn't I tell you?" I followed Jude into the kitchen and watched as she opened the fridge for what I assumed was a celebratory tub of ice cream. "When are you starting?"

"This week. And get this." She retrieved two dessertspoons and turned to face me. "I've been assigned my very own assistant. Just like you said would happen."

"That's—" I shook my head, for once lost for words, but happy, so very happy.

"Yeah. That's exactly how I reacted when they told me."

"God, that's so amazing. You'll be a star, Jude. You'll be huge."

"I hope so." She beamed at me.

We settled on the sofa and began to tuck into our chocolate chip ice cream.

"So, tell me all about it," I said.

"There's not much to tell," Jude said with a shrug. "I was introduced as *the* expert on interior design, then was asked a few questions. They liked what they saw, so they offered me the job on the spot." She was being modest; I could tell from the way her gaze kept darting across the floor, evading me. Or maybe she felt bad for progressing in her career while I was stuck with no way out. "I'll be on air five days a week for two months. Might get busy. We'll see how it goes." She smiled faintly.

"Oh, Jude." I wrapped my arms around her and pulled her close. "You have no idea how proud I am of you." And I was, big time.

"Thank you."

Was that a sniffle? I could only hope it was out of joy rather than a bad conscience.

"Want to celebrate tonight? Maybe dinner. My treat," Jude said. She *felt* bad. I cringed inwardly at the fact that she was so desperately trying to refract from her success to spare my feelings.

I shook my head. "I'm meeting Chase. Rain check?"

"Wow. Another date, huh?" Jude's gaze brushed over my clothes as though she was only now noticing that I was dressed to go out. "You two aren't wasting a second."

"He wants to talk. Nothing big," I said nonchalantly, even though my heart was beating so hard I knew she could probably smell my bluff from a mile. If she just knew how close I had been to sleeping with Chase, she would insist on celebrating. I was so sure of it; I could almost see her high-fiving the air.

Just as expected, Jude's eyebrows shot up. "About what?"

"No idea." I shrugged. "But listen. Chase and I are getting married sooner than planned."

"You're doing what?" She let out a laugh.

"He came over to tell me we'll have to do it by Tuesday. He's already arranged for the papers, so our date is fixed."

"Oh God." She leaned back, barely able to stifle her laughter. "Hanson, he's definitely not wasting time. I'll call that the blue-balls syndrome, because that's why he wants to get hitched as fast as possible. I'd gladly take a bite, if he weren't yours."

"What?" I raised my eyebrows. "You can have him." Even as I uttered those words, my pulse sped up.

"I don't think I'm his type. And frankly, you need to get laid. Like big time or else we'll have another forty-year-old virgin." She let out brief laugh. "The stars have listened to you, Laurie. I told you it was going to be a great year. All your dreams are coming true."

Gee, she was starting to sound like a fortune cookie.

"Oh please." I shook my head, smiling. "He's doing it because he has no choice."

"Because his heart tells him to?"

138

I rolled my eyes. Yeah, right. She wished. "No." I drew out the word. "Because his agent booked him a job."

Jude opened her mouth to say something, but the doorbell cut her off.

He was here.

Speak of the devil.

I brushed my hair out of my eyes nervously, wondering whether I'd ever stop being nervous around him. I figured probably soon, when I got used to his looks…and then I opened the door and my heart sank in my chest.

Holy moly.

Talk about gorgeousness.

Talk about god among gods.

How could someone as good-looking as Chase be so earthly and human?

Standing in the doorway in his shirt and blue jeans that hung low on his hips, with his dark hair and ocean-blue eyes, he was beautiful. I swallowed hard and managed a "Hi" past the lump in my throat.

"You ready?" Chase said, peering over my shoulder. I turned and noticed Jude standing there, watching us with a strange expression on her face.

"Take good care of her," she said, pointing at me. "She's a diamond and a sweetheart. I entrust you'll be good to her." She made it sound as if she was giving me away at the altar and he had to take care of me for the rest of my life.

My lips twitched, and not with amusement.

Trust Jude to be fully into this whole marriage thing, no matter how fake it was. Turning my head back to Chase, I watched his reaction, only to find my heart sinking a bit—this time for a different reason.

"I will." Chase nodded. His expression darkened just a little bit—just like it had earlier when we had been alone. Or maybe it was my imagination, because an instant later it was gone.

I squeezed into my jacket and grabbed my handbag, waving Jude goodbye. Her mouth pressed into a tight line and something crossed her features.

Concern, I realized. Maybe she didn't like Chase as much as I had figured. Or maybe she was just worried for me... Or maybe I was misreading everyone tonight.

I was slowly turning into this obsessive person who just *had* to know what everyone else thought.

"Be back soon," I mouthed to Jude. "Don't wait up."

She just nodded and closed the door.

Chapter 13

"You wanted to talk," I began as soon as we took our seats at the restaurant and the waiter had brought us the menu card.

Chase nodded gravely. "I did."

For a moment, silence fell and he looked away. A menacing vibe loomed in the air. I frowned again. His mood swings made no sense.

His hesitation told me that something bothered him and he didn't know how to communicate whatever was on his mind. I had always heard that men were broody and kind of taciturn, but I always thought Chase was the outgoing type, judging by the way he could so easily fill silence with his chatter and stories—that was all until today. Ever since his surprise visit, suspense and anxiety had followed me and I couldn't bear it anymore. I figured that if Chase had a problem, any problem at all, I better heard about it now rather than later.

"You're thinking about your ground rules. Right?" I asked slowly.

"I am." He paused again.

"Just say whatever it is, Chase. I'm not some delicate flower whose feelings you have to spare. I can handle a discussion or conflict." I leaned back, not just to regard him, but also to put more distance between us.

He looked up and a dark expression crossed his features. Slowly, he licked his lips, leaving a sparkling trail of moisture behind—the kind that made me want to press my lips against his. And then his eyes settled on me.

Dark blue and intense, and way too disconcerting.

Too intense.

My heart began to beat just a little bit harder, and a slow, delicious pull crawled between my legs.

I want him.

The thought was so vexing, my throat constricted and my hands clenched in my lap.

"Everything's been sorted out," Chase said slowly.

I narrowed my eyes on him, not getting his drift. "What's been sorted out?"

"The wedding. My friend got the necessary paperwork

done already. It's all ready for us to sign."

No hesitation. No fear. He really wanted to do it. There was just an air of nonchalance about him—and something else…that darkness again, which I couldn't quite pinpoint.

I took a deep breath and let it out slowly, looking at him with both curiosity and anticipation. "When?"

"I'll send you the details." He made it sound like a business meeting.

It's a business venture. What did you expect?

I had no idea. Maybe I didn't expect anything at all. Or maybe too much. Just not…*that*.

I crossed my legs, fidgeting in my seat uncomfortably.

"Is that what you came to tell me?" I asked. "Because if it is, you could have told me on the phone. Or at home." *When you turned up uninvited.*

He heaved a sigh, the noise of the restaurant diminishing to a soft roaring in my ears. Leaning forward, he crossed his hands over the table.

"Remember when we talked about expectations?" Chase asked slowly, ignoring my question. I shook my head, and he continued. "It was on our first date. We decided that we don't see other people while we're married."

A big, flashing neon light appeared before my eyes and a cold sensation restricted my breathing. He wanted to see other people. That was why he wanted to see me—to ask whether we could change that particular rule.

So what?

He had every right to it. I knew it. He knew it. It was to be expected in a marriage-for-hire situation. But my foolish heart took a blow nonetheless.

"If you want us to date others, I'm fine with it," I said casually, even though I didn't mean a single word. Actually, even the words—as meaningless as they were—hurt me to the core.

Chase's jaw set and his blue eyes dropped a few degrees in temperature. "That's not negotiable, Laurie. If you want to fuck, I'll be there for you."

Holy cow.

My jaw dropped, and not in a flattering way. For a few moments, all I did was stare at him as my brain fought to grasp the meaning of his words.

He didn't want me to fuck others. But what about him? Did he want to fuck me? That part he had just made pretty clear. Did he want to fuck others, too?

"You want to—" I shook my head, unable to finish the question.

Chase nodded patiently. "Everyone has needs."

Ah.

Made sense. Only, it didn't.

He made it sound like he could be available to everyone he wanted to bed while I was only allowed to have him.

"What are you saying, Chase?" My stomach turned and

my blood rushed through my veins like a swarming nest of bees—fast and dangerous.

"I'm saying that I can't control myself anymore, Laurie." His fingers closed around my hand over the table, entrapping it with his. I stared at him, both entranced by him and disgusted with myself for listening to him rather than pour a glass of water, preferably with ice cubes, on his lap. "I can't do the small things anymore."

"What small things?" I stared at him, reading his expression. And then it dawned on me. "Oh, you mean—"

"Kissing, a bit of touching here and there, you know, all the first-base things," he clarified. "Every hour I've spent in your presence so far, you've left me in painful need. I don't want to break our rules and date others, but I also don't want us to go on like this. I don't want our…" He paused, grasping for words.

"Friendship?" I suggested.

He laughed, a silky, captivating sound. "It's not friendship if we lick and suck each other, Laurie." His beautiful blue-gray gaze flickered with something and glazed over. He was thinking back to our little incident in bed. "It's called friends with benefits, only we're getting married. So we'd be a married couple with benefits."

I turned away to hide my sudden blush. A waiter came, but Chase sent him away, telling him to give us a few more minutes alone. I turned back to him, but his expression hadn't changed. He still hadn't answered my question, so I saw no other option than to ask the obvious.

"I don't understand. If you don't want me to fuck others, what about you, Chase? What do you want?"

"You know it. It's the same thing you want, Laurie." His smile disappeared. "I want to fuck you and you want me to fuck you. It's as simple as that. You see, we have quite a bit in common. At some point we'll have to go through with it."

He was right, of course.

No man could live in celibacy. At least not someone who hadn't chosen that path. Slowly, I was beginning to realize that I might be having trouble with my chosen path as well.

"If you need sex so badly, you could simply ask if you may date other women and I'll—" I shrugged, as though I didn't care, but the mere thought made me choke on my words.

He cocked his head. "Is that what you want me to do, Laurie?"

I swallowed hard. "I wouldn't have a problem with it."

I would. Very much so.

His probing glance told me he didn't believe me. "I'm asking you if that's what you want, Laurie."

"Why?" I whispered, and cleared my throat to get rid of the rasp in my voice. "Why would you even offer such a thing?" I moistened my lips, pausing. He looked at me, still as a statue, and just as beautiful. Perfect. Terrible. Frightening, even. The picture of his lips touching mine crossed my mind, soft at first, then with more fervor.

"Because the circumstances fit. It's not humanly possible for two people to spend so much time without having sex, so I want an arrangement that benefits the both of us. And there's more." His thumb began to caress my sensitive skin—the motion both innocent and fascinatingly erotic. "I want you to live with me."

My cheeks flushed with heat that traveled down my chest and settled low in the pit of my stomach.

"In the same penthouse?"

He couldn't be serious. At his meaningful stare, all blood drained from my face. I had never considered the fact that he might want to live under the same roof. Come to think of it, his wish made perfect sense, if we were to fool everyone around us. But, in my naivety, I hadn't thought so far. In fact, I hadn't thought *anything* through. Chase had been right. I hadn't planned it well enough. As if that wasn't bad enough, I hadn't even remotely anticipated how happy the thought of seeing Chase every day made me feel.

He smiled. "But those were only two requests. There's more."

My eyes snapped back to him.

"More? How many fucking demands do you have, Chase?"

"Just one more. Nothing major." He paused, and for a second his eyes lit up with amusement. "Which is understandable, considering that I also do three things for you." I raised my eyebrows as he started counting, lifting fingers as he did so. "I agreed to meet with the crazy in-laws. I agreed to marry you. And last, I agreed to teach you in all things related to sex, because you asked me to."

I stared at him. "Are you serious?"

His mouth curved in a wicked smile, sexy and mysterious. "Never been more serious. Because I agreed to help you, I want things to be fair and square. Or else you would be owing me for the rest of our lives, and I don't think you want that. Or do you, Laurie?"

Another waiter passed with a tray of drinks and Chase stopped him.

"A bottle of Krug Private Curee, please."

The waiter took his order then shuffled away silently. Chase leaned back, watching me with what I could only assume was amusement.

No, make it satisfaction. And then I realized why.

"Did you just order the most expensive champagne you could find on the menu?" I asked.

"One of the best," he replied. "We need to celebrate our new arrangement."

"I haven't agreed to anything yet."

"You have. You just haven't admitted it yet."

Oh, the arrogance.

I rolled my eyes, then cocked my head, forcing my lips to match his irritating grin. "What's the third?"

His lips twitched. "Nothing big. I just want us to stay married for a year."

Holy crap.

I stared at him, speechless. To be honest, I wasn't sure I had any blood left in me. I felt cold, and warm, excited and scared—all at the same time. At some point, my smile must have died on my lips and my jaw had dropped. I closed it but still didn't manage to utter a word.

Chase was still grinning, his eyes boring into me, enjoying every second. Finally the air whooshed out of me, but still no words stumbled out. My tongue stuck to the back of my throat and my mind remained surprisingly blank. At last, the waiter appeared with the bottle of champagne and filled our flutes, then disappeared again, oblivious to the turmoil inside me.

I grabbed the flute and took a full sip, then another, the delicious taste barely registering in my brain. For all I cared, he could have ordered tap water and I wouldn't even have noticed the difference.

"Is this some kind of joke?" I finally asked.

"No joke. I would never embarrass or ridicule you,

Laurie. Those are my conditions. Sex. Living together. And staying married for a whole year. You either agree or we can't get married."

Holy shit.

I narrowed my eyes. "Are you blackmailing me?"

He cringed visibly, as though even the idea was beyond him. "Call it an offer. A demand, maybe, but one that will benefit the both of us, like I said before."

He lifted his flute and motioned me to raise mine. "Those are my terms. Take it or leave it," Chase continued, unfazed by my sudden silence and the dread gripping my heart.

"A year," I said feebly. A year of seeing him on a daily basis, sleeping next door, maybe even sleeping with him, if he so desired. Somewhere I could hear something burst— my stupid bubble and hope of annulling our marriage within twenty-four hours. "Do I even have a say in that matter?"

"We could pretend you do."

My breath hitched in my throat, but this time not from dread. I realized, as much as I was terrified, the idea appealed to me.

"I don't know," I muttered, ignoring his glass of champagne. "I've never lived with anyone before and I don't know what you expect."

He shrugged, lowering his arm, and took a sip of his

champagne, before leaning back, more relaxed than I had ever seen him.

"That's pretty simple. I'm not a man of many demands, which is why I have jotted them down for future reference." He reached into the briefcase at his feet and pulled out an envelope, then pushed it across the table toward me. "Here's everything you need to know. Take a look when you get home and tell me what you think. If you want to negotiate, I'm open to suggestions, though I'm not going to budge on those three terms, as mentioned."

"I thought I was hiring you. I didn't realize you had expectations," I said feebly, my heart sinking in my chest. Of course, in order to hire his services I would have to pay him. Given that I was struggling in the financial department and he was doing me a favor, it made sense that he expected something in return.

"Of course I do. Everyone has expectations, or else we would be taken for granted or taken advantage of," Chase said.

He made himself sound so weak and innocent, I had to suppress a snarky reply.

"Taken advantage of, huh?"

"You asked me how you could repay me, and those are my requests. There is no such thing as a free ride. I'll just go on and call it fair." He tipped his long finger against the envelope. "Like I said, everything you need to know is in there."

My fingers clasped around the envelope, fidgeting, as my curiosity got a hold of me, urging me to find out what those requests were. Chase's hand settled on mine again and squeezed lightly. "At home, Laurie."

His voice was soft, maybe carrying even the slightest hint of a gentle, romantic undertone. Judging by the way his hand lingered on me and his eyes were glinting, anyone watching would think he had just proposed to me.

And he had.

But people would have been surprised at what he had just offered.

"It's an indecent proposal, Chase," I whispered.

He tilted his head. "I have to agree, but I can promise you it's one you'll appreciate." He winked. "Now we're going to enjoy our dinner and talk about something else. It's our third and last date before our marriage, so I want it to be good and decent, because after Tuesday, it will be nothing of that sort."

All words inside my brain died. I had no idea what he meant, but maybe it didn't matter—for the time being.

He waved at the waiter to take our order. I pushed the envelope aside unwillingly, but my mind kept circling around the question at hand.

What exactly did he expect in return for his favors?

Chapter 14

Our date barely lasted half an hour. When I arrived back home, Jude was waiting in the living room with countless boxes scattered around her and a phone cradled between her ear and shoulder. I peered through the door to say hi, ignoring the mess scattered all over the floor, and then headed for my bedroom, locking the door behind me. The last thing I needed was for her to pop in at an unfortunate moment. Not that I had anything to hide from her, but whatever Chase's envelope contained, I wanted the privacy to look it over without anyone's input. Revealing intimate details about my life wasn't really my thing, and I had a feeling that Chase's demands were more than that. Plus, the suspense was killing me. Not knowing about something was almost worse than dying of boredom.

Sitting on my bed, I peeled the envelope open and pulled out two sheets of paper. It was an agreement.

I stared in disbelief at rows and rows of words—all Chase's wishes—and then began to read, unable to stop the heat spreading through me.

Like Chase had announced, his first demand was that we remained married for a whole year, during which we would live in the same household, albeit in different bedrooms. He also expected me to relocate to NYC for the next few weeks and move in with him straight away, because he had to work there.

I could deal with that.

And NYC sounded exciting. It had always been at the top of my 'places to visit' list.

A few points suited the purpose of resolving everyday issues, like financial arrangements. He preferred to keep his financial status a secret, and so did I. He expected me to accompany him to social gatherings and support him in his career, which was to be expected given that he was an actor. Hanging out with the right people was probably part of the job description.

So far, so good.

I could do that.

I liked to be professional.

What cut off my air supply was the next point on his list.

Or, to be more precise, the few points that centered around sex.

Holy cow!

What the hell were some of those words? I knew Chase wanted to get down and dirty with me, but what the fuck! He had compiled a whole list of things he wanted to teach me. They were so bad, heat began to travel through me and settle in places I didn't want to be reminded of.

Chase's requirement of using safe words didn't help either.

I rubbed a hand over my eyes and then reread the few points in the hope I might have misinterpreted the obvious, but no matter how often I analyzed his words, the requirements remained the same:

He wanted experimental sex.

Why do you act surprised, Hanson? He told you that before.

Yeah, he had. I just couldn't wrap my head around the word 'experimental.'

During dinner he had offered to sleep with me should I so desire in the future. Only, my brain hadn't quite grasped the full meaning of his words.

That sex wasn't just sex.

That it involved intimacy, and getting really close to someone.

That there were different kinds of sex, and judging from Chase's words, he wanted adventure, passion, the whole shebang, with different levels and a variety of activities.

I frowned, because Chase hadn't just offered. His agreement stated that he expected me to do the deed within a week of the wedding ceremony, which would mean that in less than one week I wasn't just going to be his wife.

In less than a week, I'd sleep with him.

I swallowed hard.

At least Chase had specified that I had a say in the time and choice of place. And because different people had different needs and he didn't know how often I'd want him—his exact words—we'd have to do a few runs to find out.

I turned the paper over, and as I read on, I stumbled on one paragraph.

I frowned and my eyes widened.

Holy cow.

He expected sex at least twice a week during the entire time we remained married.

What the hell!

I shook my head in disbelief.

Twice a week for one year.

A year had fifty-two weeks, which meant I would have to fuck him—how many times?

I leaned forward and buried my head in my hands.

Oh, God.

At least a hundred and four times within one year. And

since—from the look of it—Chase was into experimental, he probably harbored every intention of covering the entire *Kama Sutra*.

Talk about demanding.

Everyone has needs, Hanson. It's natural.

Only Chase had a whole bunch of them. As he had said, "We both need it."

I figured by that he had meant that *he* had needs and it was my duty as his wife to fulfill them. I drew a long breath and let it out slowly as I pushed the paper back into the envelope, my mind spinning with unwanted pictures: Chase holding me, his lips descending upon mine, his hands roaming over my body, touching places no one had touched before him, his finger playing with my folds, rubbing my clit, before he shredded the last mystery of my bodily needs.

Heat crept up my neck, which intensified as my cell phone began to ring and I stared at the caller ID.

Speak of the devil.

Instantly, my heart started to hammer against my chest. Against my better judgment, I looked over my shoulder to make sure he wasn't standing there, watching me—which was impossible, given that the door was locked and I would have heard someone entering.

As much as I didn't want to talk to him now, what difference did it make? Sooner or later I'd have to talk with him about all the things I couldn't agree to.

Chapter 15

I smoothed a hand over my clothes and sat up straight, because, even though he couldn't see me, I figured he might be able to tell my state of mind from my voice.

"Hi," I said, picking up on the third ring, infusing as much boredom into my voice as was possible.

"Did you read it, Laurie?" came Chase's reply.

No beating around the bush.

His voice was deep and deliciously sexy. Something stirred in me at the way my name rolled on his tongue, sending a light tremble through my core, and making my breathing harder. Was that his usual telephone voice? Or just the one he put on when he talked to women?

"Yes." I grimaced at how hoarse my voice sounded.

"And?"

What did he expect me to say? I hesitated. If I accepted his demands so quickly, he'd always think I was a pushover. But could I really go through a round of negotiation without dying of sheer mortification? Could I really talk matter-of-factly about all the things I had no experience of and was not comfortable talking about?

"You really want me to relocate to New York and live with you?" I asked, slightly out of breath.

"Yes. It's just for a couple of weeks."

"I don't know, Chase. While I understand your points, your stipulations aren't really what I signed up for when I offered you the job." I made sure to emphasize the word *job*, because in the end I was the employer, and consequently I was supposed to be the one formulating the demands.

"What do you suggest?" Chase asked.

He was willing to listen. That was good. In fact, very good.

I needed cooperation. For him to come halfway or maybe bend to my rules.

Yeah, he was the one who had to do the bending.

Will against will.

I could win that one.

I bit my lip as my mind began to put together my own list. I couldn't *possibly* live with him while fighting this stupid attraction. I was already having troubles kicking him out of my mind.

"I'm fine with staying married and living together for a month or two, during which we sleep in separate bedrooms," I started. "After the month is over we claim to have different work schedules, and because you're away on jobs, it's necessary that we stay in separate apartments."

Silence.

I waited a few seconds.

The line was so quiet I wasn't sure he hadn't hung up.

"Chase?"

"That's not going to work for me," Chase said at last. "Come to think of it, I'm not so keen on the different bedrooms idea either."

Oh, God. He couldn't be serious. My heart sank in my chest.

He's playing you, Hanson.

"Take it or leave it," I said through gritted teeth.

"You need this more than I do, Laurie. Think about it. I could as well have asked for payment, you know, but I didn't. So, I won't change my requests."

The line went dead.

What the fuck?

He had hung up on me.

Again.

My blood began to boil in my veins.

Who the heck did he think he was?

Yes, gorgeous was his middle name, and yes, his claim that I needed him carried some truth. But what the hell! I wasn't going to let a man dictate *my* business proposition. Not when I was the one who should have been holding all the strings.

Breathing hard, I counted to ten, forcing myself to calm down.

I managed to let my ego control my reasoning for all of five seconds, after which I dialed his number.

"Fine," I mumbled. "We live together."

"In my house. For one year."

Given that my home was a tiny rented apartment with barely enough space to accommodate Jude's extensive wardrobe and shoe collection, Chase's suggestion wasn't such a bad idea.

"Okay. But I have to insist on different rooms, if we're to live together." I closed my eyes, mentally willing him to give in, because this one was my no-negotiation area. He was asking the impossible.

I simply couldn't let him stay in the same room with me.

The line went silent again, but I still could hear his breathing.

"I need my privacy, Chase."

He remained silent for a long moment, probably considering whether he could push his luck with this one. I rolled my eyes and kicked at the pillow with my foot.

"I mean it, Chase," I whispered. "If I don't get my privacy, then I cannot do this." *And you know I need those letters*, I added mentally. If not to discover the truth, then at least to find peace and bury the past once and for all.

I bit my lip hard until I thought the thin layer of skin might tear. The other end of the line continued to remain quiet, and for a moment I feared Chase had hung up on me again.

And then he spoke.

"Why?" His voice came low, strangled.

Why?

There were so many reasons. Like the fact that I wasn't ready to share my bed or life or anything at all with a man. Or the fact that if we slept in the same room I might not be strong enough to resist his advances or looks. I just had to remind myself of the last time we had been in his bed, and of how close I had been to giving in, to know that I couldn't cave on this one. And then there was the fact that I had never been attracted to anyone like this before, which wasn't bad per se. But with new territories come new experiences and new challenges. Chase was such a challenge…a challenge I knew instinctively I couldn't win. Like with all new things, the prospect of entering new and uncharted territories scared me. But how could I explain this to someone who wouldn't understand?

"It's just not a possibility," I said.

"Trust me, Laurie." Chase spoke with a casual familiarity, as though he could sense the storm wreaking havoc within me. Maybe he thought he knew me, concluding that I had been hurt in the past. Or maybe his words were nothing but empty shells, spoken to other women countless times.

I shook my head, even though he couldn't see me.

Marriage? Yes, for a reason, and for that reason only. Trust? Impossible.

"I cannot do that," I said. "And I don't care if you understand. This is all I can say."

"All right." He sighed. "Different rooms, then." Did I detect a hint of disappointment in his voice?

Your imagination's running wild, Hanson.

I smirked. So true, and not just in this instance. I kept imagining things. Things he wanted to say but didn't. Things I wanted to say and do but could never admit. Things that made me blush even in his absence, out of fear that he might just be able to sense my forbidden desires…and act upon them.

"Okay. One more time, just to make sure you got it. We live together, but we'll have different rooms," I repeated, in the hope my tone carried enough determination that he wouldn't try to change his mind later.

"Yes."

I heaved an exaggerated sigh, ready to move on to my next point in the agreement, but Chase's voice pricked my bubble.

"But I still expect you to stay married for one year. One year, Laurie," he said. "We can sleep in separate rooms, but I expect our relationship to be exclusive, and for me to teach you. I won't accept any arguing or bargaining on this point. Deal?"

I stared at the sheets, completely overwhelmed. What relationship would that be?

"What if it doesn't work out?" I asked.

"Why shouldn't it?" He sounded annoyed. Suddenly I could picture him clearly in my mind, his brow furrowed and his jaw clenching.

"People get divorced all the time, you know, even when they're in love." *And we're not*, I wanted to add, but didn't. "They make mistakes and realize maybe the other one isn't all they hoped for. One year can be a very long time."

"If there's a problem, we'll talk about it and can renegotiate our terms. But until then, I see absolutely no reason for discussing what might never be."

I brushed a hand through my hair nervously. "Okay. I'm in."

There, I'd said it.

No chance to take it back.

"All right." His voice softened. "Make sure to sign the

contract."

"All right," I repeated.

There was a short silence before Chase spoke again, "Have you thought about the kind of wedding you want?"

He was changing the subject, avoiding the one thing I had no choice but to discuss.

"Whatever we do works for me," I whispered. "Make an appointment with a justice of the peace and I'll be there."

"I have already done that. Do you have a paper and pen?"

"One sec."

I opened my appointment book and flicked through the blank pages, my mood darkening, until I reached the page that said Tuesday. Chase confirmed the date and time with me.

I was really doing it.

It was really happening.

The thoughts of my imminent wedding made my head spin, as I realized just how soon it'd all be.

Too soon.

"Laurie?" Chase's voice cut through the silence.

For once I wished I could see him, catch his reaction, know what he was doing.

"Is this a really a good idea?" I whispered, my voice almost breaking.

"Are you getting cold feet already? We haven't even

reached the altar yet." His voice carried a hint of amusement. And then laughter erupted. "Laurie, I won't ask impossible things from you. I'm just trying to help us both."

"You don't understand," I mumbled. "Those things you expect of me, I'm not sure I can do them." I eyed the sheets again, his words ringing in my mind loud and clear. "What if I don't like it? Or what if I just can't?"

"We'll take it one step at a time and find out what you like and what you don't. But make no mistake, Laurie. I won't hurt you or force myself on you. And I sure won't do things you won't like. Experimental sex is what it is—us trying to find our heights and limits…" He trailed off, leaving the rest to my imagination. "Trust me."

Maybe Chase was right.

"Do you have any other questions, Laurie? Anything that still bothers you? We'll soon be a couple, so you need to be honest with me." The humor was back. In spite of the seriousness of the situation, I found myself smiling.

Was I ready to reveal my real thoughts?

My neck prickled and burned, as though I had just been stung by a jellyfish.

I had to.

"About the other thing. The day of our wedding." I paused and moistened my lips as I pulled my legs to my chest. "How will our day look like?"

"We won't have time to arrange something elaborate," Chase explained. "Maybe a reception, have dinner, and then we could spend the night in a hotel."

My stomach churned.

"Chase," I said sharply. "Just so we're on the same page, I'm not going to spend a minute in a hotel unless we have separate rooms."

"Yeah, I know. You've made yourself clear on the issue." Disappointment again, with just a hint of anger. Or maybe it wasn't anger so much as indignation.

He thinks you're rejecting him, which is understandable. First, you told him he was welcome. And then you said you didn't want to sleep in the same room.

Talk about complicated.

"Whatever," I muttered, and tucked my legs beneath me as I prepared myself to fight my corner. "I'm not going to sleep with you on Tuesday. That's way too soon."

"Are you sure about that?" No hesitation. No indignation. Just pure male arrogance. I had been wrong. He didn't think I was rejecting him. He was convinced I could never say no and consequently he was impatient to take what he thought I'd give him sooner or later anyway.

I would *never* sleep with him; not because I didn't want to, but just to spite him. Someone had to put a dent in that arrogance of his. The last time I found myself in bed with him, I had dropped my panties for him. My mistake. I had been too preoccupied with how sexy he looked, instead of realizing the kind of danger his good looks had on me, and what that could mean for us.

That was all before Chase came up with the sordid suggestion of living together.

Now I had to step up my game.

But keeping my panties on had never felt more difficult.

No pressure at all.

"Sleeping with you would be a conflict of interest, and you know it. Scratch the wedding night sex part or I'm out," I said coldly.

"Fine. If you're not interested in sex now, we don't have to do anything." His voice was nonchalant—cold, even. "Sooner or later, you'll want me anyway. You told me before and you'll do it again. There's no doubt about that."

No, he hadn't just said it!

I laughed, but the sound came out all weak and strangled. Truth was, I had never met anyone like him and his self-assurance. The fact that he was so sure I'd accept all his wishes and demands frightened me.

"We'll see about that," I said, surprised by how defensive I sounded.

"Absolutely," Chase replied, his tone still cold. "But just so you know, I'm not a man to beg. I'm a man to take. I'll make sure you know what you're missing out on until you come begging me for it…again."

My breath hitched in my throat and my heart began to hammer in my ears.

He's only looking for a fun ride.

I shook my head, plucking at the fringes of my pillow.

Most men I had met thought they were only a training session away from an Armani model, which had always amused me. I could deal with an overinflated ego that was based on no merits at all. What I couldn't deal with was a guy who actually had it all in the looks department. Chase wasn't just all sexy, raunchy maleness. He had known which buttons to press to make me come so hard I couldn't wait to do it again. Chase was pure uncorrupted perfection designed to corrupt my soul. One night with him and he might turn me from a tame cat into a tigress, and that I couldn't afford.

"Don't be so sure about that. Maybe you should have taken up my offer when you had your chance." The words came out before I could stop them.

"I agree, because then we wouldn't be having this conversation. You'd be lying beneath me, panting my name." He sounded amused. "I don't want to brag, but I bet you'll be doing a lot of that once we get started."

Chase had made himself pretty clear on that point. Only, on our first meeting, when he had put all the cards on the table, I hadn't realized he had made it with the intention of pursuing a physical relationship with me later. I hadn't even realized that he was the kind to carry his promises through.

There'll be plenty of time for that in one year.

I still couldn't wrap my mind around that one.

For a second we both fell silent. I bit my lip again as my brain fought hard to come up with a good excuse to end the conversation.

"Whatever you do, babe"—I cringed at his choice of words—"I expect to see you at the wedding ceremony."

"I didn't think you were serious on that part. That's in four days."

"Did I mention we're getting married in NYC and we'll be staying?"

I frowned. "Already? But you said your job—"

"The sooner we move, the better," he said, cutting me off. "Don't miss your flight."

Oh, God.

"Why didn't you say that earlier?" I whispered, and rolled my eyes. "I need to go, Chase," I said weakly. "There's a lot to do."

"I'll come over tonight and help you pack."

Hell no!

I'd had enough of his complex mood swings, ranging from cold to sweet to angry and intensely sexual. I could deal with complex. But unpredictable was a whole other world.

"No need. Jude's here."

"The more the merrier," Chase said. "I'll bring dinner and a bottle of wine."

Why hadn't I come up with a better excuse? Like having a date or yoga class?

"I don't drink."

"Are you sure? Because as far as I remember, and please feel free to correct me if I'm wrong, you seemed to like it a lot at the restaurant."

I had *known* he'd bring that up eventually. Brushing imaginary dust from the pillow, I said, "That was a one-off, okay? I was stressed."

"One-off, huh? Just like all the other things, right?" Chase laughed. "We'll have to find you a new way to relieve stress, because obviously, you have a denial mechanism going on there, Laurie. I have a few things in mind that we could try together. It's all rather Tantric."

There it was again.

Only this time I knew I hadn't been imagining things from his hoarse voice. My cheeks caught fire at his insinuation. And more so when my brain began to come up with its own interpretation of all the things Chase and I could try out together.

A sense of longing settled between my legs, pulsating to life.

Before he could answer, I peeled my cell phone off my ear and switched it off, then threw it on the bed in exasperation.

I rubbed my throbbing temples.

This whole marriage thing was going to be a disaster, and Chase might end up being a huge pain in the ass. I just knew it. Or else why did he have to be so irritably and annoyingly pushy and insist on an agreement that benefited mostly him?

But only mostly!

If only I could switch off the annoying voice in the back of my mind that gushed about how hot Chase was and how much I wanted to feel him inside of me. That I should celebrate a new, sexual stage in my life and everything that came with it, because I might just like it more than I wanted him to know.

I wasn't afraid of a little intimacy. I wasn't afraid of getting married. Or even moving to NYC. But living together in the same apartment, seeing Chase day after day? Staying married for one year, not being able to dodge him and his sexy body?

Horrendous.

Imagine all the self-control needed.

However, I liked him. The thought of seeing him every day for the next twelve months was ridiculously appealing.

I liked having him close.

With a sigh, I grabbed the pen, and before I could change my mind, I signed the contract, then leaned back, excited.

Of course, I could only hope he'd keep his promise and not insist that we share a bed. And what if Chase was untidy, leaving his socks or underwear in the bathroom, and I'd begin to hate him for it?

I shuddered.

But the prospect of dealing with difficulties along the way had never put me off. In fact, now that I had seen how Chase ticked, I was convinced I could take on his self-assurance and arrogance, maybe even change him—tame him. Someone had to...for his own good.

And then there was me—I wanted to explore, to experience things with him.

"Jude?" I opened the door and yelled down the hall.

"What?" came her voice.

"Guess what? I need you to help me pack. Apparently I'm moving in with my future husband."

Chapter 16

How had I gotten myself into this mess?

That question was all I could think of as the weekend and Monday passed in a blur. For the thousandth time, I checked my phone. Chase hadn't called.

Except for a simple text on Sunday, which informed me that he had received the signed contract and that we'd meet in New York, I heard nothing else from him.

Nothing at all, which left a sore feeling inside my heart that annoyed me.

I was not supposed to be disappointed.

What was even more stupid was the fact that, at some point, I had started to miss him. Crazy, not least because I'd be seeing him in less than twelve hours. But the knowledge only ended up increasing the unnerving sense of longing and anticipation.

The thing was, in spite of my anger at Chase for turning everything around to suit him, and taking control of the situation, I couldn't stay mad at him. My anger evaporated the window the moment Clint called to check in and enquire whether I was indeed getting married.

God, how much I disliked him, the controlling son of a bitch. It had taken every ounce of my willpower not to tell my stepfather to shove his fake concern up his ass. Without him, I would never have been in the kind of situation I had found myself in. I would have inherited my mom's belongings, not have to get married to get a bunch of stupid letters.

At last, Casey called to confirm that our dresses were ready (big thanks to her grandmother sensing we needed them earlier), and Jude picked them up just in time.

They were now neatly packed in a plastic bag, ready to be draped over our arms. In spite of Jude's insistence, I couldn't even force myself to try my wedding gown on. I couldn't even pull it out and see if the customized copy was as beautiful as the original Vera Wang.

Chase did that to me.

All his requests, every reminder, every thought about him, had me in turmoil. I was sure I was making a big mistake, until Jude reminded me of the purpose of everything.

It was a sacrifice I had to make. For myself. For my mom. To get those letters, because it was the only way for me to have them.

Without them, I would have run—far away, if only to escape Chase's sexy charm and the things he seemed to stir inside me. He had something no man possessed. It was the glint in his eyes, the smoothness of his voice when he talked, and the genuine concern in his tone, that made me feel like I was the only person on earth. As much as I wanted to avoid him for the rest of my life, there was a part of me that looked forward to it.

I wanted to spend more time with Chase.

I wanted it all to be real.

I cringed at those words.

Stupid, stupid thoughts.

They were nothing but trouble, with the sole purpose of confusing me. Like those unwanted and annoying emotions I wanted to switch off but couldn't.

I smiled to Jude, even though I knew I could never reveal to her the extent of the feelings I was slowly developing for Chase. I wasn't even sure what they were. I wasn't in love per se. It was lust, longing, a need that only he could fulfill. And yes, I really liked Chase, even though I had no clue what exactly it was that pulled me to him, besides his good looks.

The demands he had at the last minute not only took me by surprise—they shocked me. I had always assumed that Chase would go along with my plans and expectations, not that he'd use the opportunity to take control. It made me wonder if Jude's words about me being relationship material might just be correct, or why else would Chase be so hellbent on dragging out the entire marriage thing, which could hurt us both and end in more disappointment than I could handle?

At dawn on Monday, it was time to move. My two suitcases were packed to the brim—enough stuff for the next few weeks, or as long as I'd be staying in New York City. With a last glance at my apartment building, I stepped into the waiting taxi. The sadness at leaving my old life behind had made room for slight anticipation.

I couldn't wait to see Chase again.

A little later, I boarded the plane to NYC—with Jude—because my fiancé had decided to fly ahead for a last-minute job and then meet me at the wedding venue.

His text message had read, *Got a job. See you there. xxx*

Proverbially speaking, he was killing two birds with one stone.

Made sense.

I would probably have done the same thing because—fake fiancé or not—who in their right mind wanted to see the future spouse surrounded by all the wedding stress? But the knowledge didn't quite manage to dissolve my jealousy at the prospect of Chase kissing another woman for a scene; or shooting some magazine cover, his strong arms wrapped around the half-naked body of an exotic female model with sky-high legs and sun-kissed skin.

What had enraged me even more was the fact that after our strange phone conversation on Friday, he couldn't be bothered to even wish me a pleasant flight. On Sunday, while I was in the shower, he had simply dropped off my plane ticket, a hotel reservation, and a brochure of the wedding venue, and then sent said text message.

The big day had now arrived.

Tucking my bridal gown under one arm while clutching at my trolley and maneuvering my way through the early-afternoon crowd at JFK airport in NYC, I could have screamed from frustration. I had never seen so many people crammed in one place. Luckily for me, Jude was here to provide a welcome diversion.

"Think he'll turn up?" she asked as soon as we had taken our seat in a cab and had instructed the driver to take us to our hotel.

I grimaced and turned away so she wouldn't catch my dark expression. "Honestly, I don't know."

"If he doesn't, I'll marry you." She squeezed my hand and pursed her lips to send me an air kiss. The driver regarded us in the rearview mirror and I laughed, imagining the dirty direction his thoughts had probably taken.

In the end, all men had one thing in common, and it wasn't the ability to stay committed or faithful.

Sex.

Three simple letters.

That was all Chase would ever want from me, just like every other man I had ever gone out with. None of them had scored and neither would Chase, or at least not without me mentally putting up a good fight—like keeping the hell away from him, and—most importantly—avoiding being alone with him at all costs. Even if he truly wanted us to be exclusive throughout our marriage, jumping into bed with him was out of the question, because—

I drew a sharp breath and blew it out slowly as I remembered just how much I had wanted it—when I hadn't felt pressured. The moment Chase made his demands, the walls came down and I felt pushed into a position I didn't want to be in. I couldn't just blame him. It was the entire situation that scared the crap out of me. The whole marriage thing in order to get those letters and feeling threatened by Clint was a complete turn-off.

But as I sat in the taxi, my eyes scanning over the amazing views that only NYC could offer, my mind began to come up with a list of reasons in favor of a physical relationship with Chase. As much as I abhorred the fact that I was attracted to him, there was no point in denying it.

But where there's a physical relationship, there's also emotional entanglement. Seeing that I had already developed feelings for Chase, I didn't want them to deepen and take a dangerous turn for my heart. I didn't want to invest too much. I had no idea what the future held in store for me, but whatever it was, feelings had a tendency to make everything more complicated than it needed to be.

Some things just couldn't happen for our own good—regardless of whether Chase was amazing or not—and Chase was, just too much for my liking.

"No fucking way," Jude said, pointing out the window and tugging at my shirt at the same time.

Realizing the car must have stopped at some point, I turned to follow Jude's line of vision and my jaw dropped.

Holy shit.

Was that even real?

The driver had pulled over in front of the most magnificent hotel I had ever seen, and that included anything I had ever seen in the movies. It was huge, decorated with a glass front that sparkled in the midmorning sun. Luxurious, carved marble flowerpots had been arranged on either side of a red carpet, and uniformed service personnel wearing white gloves stood outside, completely motionless, like in an old black-and-white movie.

"I thought you were broke," Jude whispered, pointing

her head to the grand place, as I paid the driver and exited the car.

"I am," I said dryly. "This is all Chase's doing. He said he reserved a place for us."

"You're lucky he's rich," Jude whispered.

"Don't say that." I scowled. "You know that's exactly what I *didn't* want him to be."

"Either he didn't get the memo that you're broke, or it's all paid for because he can, and he'll expect his reward afterward. Like tomorrow night." Jude's eyes gleamed as she glanced at the huge water fountain. As though anyone could possibly misinterpret her badly disguised insinuation, Jude turned her head to me and raised her brows meaningfully.

My cheeks caught fire under her scrutiny. She had no idea how close she had come to the truth. For once I was happy she didn't know about our agreement. Or how close Chase and I had already come to having sex. Or his crazy demands.

"Well, which one do you think it is, Hanson?" Jude asked, her eyes narrowed. "Is it all a gift, a favor— something a friend with money would do for you with no strings? Or will he insist on collecting his prize, reward, or whatever he'll call it, when he feels like it?"

"I honestly have no idea," I mumbled in the hope she'd just shut up. "Let's hope it's the first one, because he can't

181

have anything else without first consulting me."

Or he could just make me owe him.

Again.

"I bet it's the latter." Jude grinned. "Whether he's paid for it all or not, you're lucky. He's not only rich, he wants you so bad, it's obvious that he's totally into you, ready to sweep you off your feet, as soon you as you enter his bedroom."

"I'm not sure about that."

Did he want to sleep with me because he liked me, or because I was some sort of prize—the one woman who hadn't immediately dropped her panties for him? That was the question I had been asking myself for a while, and this new development had made me none the wiser.

I could only guess that he sort of liked me. I had no sexual experience, but Chase and I had a connection. There was no denying that. I felt it when I touched him. I could see it in the way he looked at me before his lips brushed mine. But would he go as far as paying so that I owed him and had to repay him eventually? It was hard to believe, but I would find out soon enough.

The real question was, was I really ready to know the truth?

Shrugging, irritated, I diverted my attention to the man in a black uniform who hurried over to help us with the luggage. I shot him a thankful smile, both for his assistance and for unknowingly rescuing me from Jude's inquisition, and followed him down the red carpet, through a pair of massive glass doors, and into the hotel lobby. In spite of its modern exterior, the interior design told a completely different story. Gigantic glass chandeliers were mirrored in the polished cream marble floors, which built a stunning contrast to the wine-red divans and abstract art paintings. The place smelled of the upper class, both those born into old money and those sleeping their way to the top. Dressed in blue jeans and a loose asymmetrical top, I had never felt so out of place as Jude and I approached the reception desk to sign in.

The receptionist, a friendly guy in his early forties, barely looked at us before handing us our room swipe cards, together with a brochure on the hotel's facilities.

"Please feel free to call us if you need anything, ma'am." He smiled, flashing unnaturally bright teeth. "It will be our pleasure to provide you with the best service you could wish for."

"Thanks," I said, and held out my credit card with shaky fingers, praying that Chase had thought of placing reservations for the cheapest rooms available.

"No need, miss." The receptionist shook his head politely. "It's already paid for. Mr. Wright has already taken care of everything."

My stomach flipped.

Somewhere to my right I thought I heard Jude snorting, but I didn't dare turn to regard her, knowing too well the kind of look she'd probably throw me.

"Thanks," I said again, only this time the words barely made it past my lips.

Chase *knew* I couldn't afford staying in this kind of place and yet he hadn't even thought about checking in with me before making a reservation and—

Now I owed him for that, too.

I turned my head away from Jude, my neck pricking from her inquisitive stare.

Damn!

He was taking control again—and not in a way I liked. He wasn't that bad when he followed my commands and tried to please me. But the moment he became all stubborn and unreasonable, I had no idea how to deal with him.

Chapter 17

This whole marriage thing wasn't starting the way I had envisioned it at all. I couldn't take anything from a man, and certainly not from someone like Chase, and so I vowed to pay him back. As we walked the expensively furnished hall, my eyes taking in the rich and upper-class people dressed in their designer attire, my mouth went dry at the thought of paying Chase back.

Oh, God.

Did he *have* to book us into what looked like one of the most expensive hotels in the state? It was supposed to be just a ten-minute ceremony, where we signed a few papers, and then we were done. Not spending a night in the kind of place that would most certainly break the bank if I kept true to my conviction and footed the bill myself.

"Come on. You need to lie down before you faint on the spot." Jude's hand clasped around my upper arm and she pulled me to the elevator area. Behind us I could hear the receptionist communicating our room numbers and instructing someone to bring our luggage up and show us the way, but I didn't look back. All I did was follow Jude's command as we were shown our way to our rooms, my stomach turning to ice.

The elevator came to a halt on one of the lower floors. The bellboy opened the door and stepped aside to let us in.

I breathed a sigh of relief. At least Chase hadn't gone for the most expensive room. Deep down I knew he would have understood how awkward it would have been for me if he had done that.

The room was pretty, consisting of a neat double bed, large TV, a desk, a tiny walk-in closet, and an exquisite bathroom. Nothing more, and yet everything I would have expected from this kind of hotel. With another relieved sigh, I dropped my handbag on the bed when I noticed the bellboy frowning.

Of course, I still had to tip him, stupid me.

Absentmindedly, I held out a twenty-dollar note to tip him before he left, and then I noticed my suitcases behind him, outside in the hall.

"Your suite's on the top floor, ma'am," he said in thick

New York accent. "Please follow me."

The penny dropped. "Wait, did you just say suite?"

"Yes, ma'am," he said, and for a moment I thought I recognized a spark of panic in his eyes. "It's the best we have. Mr. Wright wanted the presidential suite, but it was already booked. I'm sorry for any inconvenience caused, but you'll find our executive suite offers a truly VIP experience and…" The rushing in my ears muffled his voice.

Oh my God.

My face paled at the realization that Chase had asked for the most expensive room in the hotel. No expenses spared. The initial bad feeling had blossomed into a full-blown itch on my skin. I didn't even dare to look to Jude, knowing that she was probably inwardly laughing her head off.

"Ma'am?" The bellboy's voice drew me back to reality. I glanced at him and realized he was waiting for me.

I nodded, but didn't move from the spot.

Would he find me rude if I announced that I'd be staying with Jude?

"I'll be fine. Go. I'll see you later," Jude whispered. Before she turned away, I caught her smile, which was supposed to be comforting, even though the twitching of her lips implied that she was having a hard time not laughing.

I couldn't blame her. The situation would have been

hilarious—and just a little bit romantic—were it not happening to me.

Holding my head high, I grabbed my bag and followed the bellboy back to the elevator, suppressing all my conflicting emotions—most of which were urging me to call a taxi and return to L.A.

My heart hammered hard as we reached the first door on the top floor and the bellboy opened it, his easygoing chatter all the while amplifying my initial assumption that Chase had spent a whole lot of money on something that should have been of no importance to both of us.

I stepped into a wide hall that led into a living room with state-of-the-art furniture and floor-to-ceiling glass windows, more confused than before. This didn't look like any suite I had ever seen.

It was far too big and luxurious for that. But then again, I hadn't slept in many suites in my life. From the plush bedding, French doors, and the beautiful, warm décor to the expensive carpets and rich draperies, everything screamed style and elegance. It looked so darn expensive, they should have charged for viewings.

"If you don't like it, we'll be happy to offer you something more suitable for your needs," the bellboy offered, misinterpreting my deadly silence and cranky gaze.

Damn right I wasn't happy. I had wanted *affordable*, not yet another invisible reminder of my low credit score. But, as angry as I was, I wasn't going to make a scene. It wasn't the poor bellboy's fault that Chase was driving me crazy with his unnerving way of showing off. Forget crazy. He was driving me insane, and not in that 'screaming his name in the waves of lust' kind of way.

"It's great," I forced myself to say through clenched teeth. "Thank you."

"If you need anything, we'll be happy to assist you. The suite comes with a twenty-four-hour in-room dining experience that includes champagne service."

What the fuck was champagne service?

I listened as he explained a few more things and then he left. Completely exhausted, I slumped down on a chair near the fireplace and looked around, still incredulous.

What the hell had Chase been thinking when he booked a suite for me?

That I'd need it to host a dinner party just for myself?

I buried my head in my hands. The suite probably had at least two bedrooms. Plenty of space. For what? Once I closed my eyes at night, I might as well sleep in a storage room and not know it. What a complete waste of money! Didn't Chase ever learn how to save up and put it all to good use?

You're blowing it all out of proportion.

I knew I was, but the knowledge didn't change the way I felt.

Chase had meant to be generous, but I knew there had to be a different reason for his charity.

I knew men like Chase—seemingly generous on the outside, but there were always hidden intentions, always demands that would surface later.

Because nothing was ever free.

Not this time.

I had every intention of repaying him. And I'd tell him the moment I'd see him.

A crack, followed by a thud, jerked me out of my thoughts. I jumped up, startled, and caught movement from the corner of my eye.

Someone was here. Outside, in the hall.

My heart began to beat unnaturally fast, imitating the speed of the racing thoughts inside my head. An intruder? No, it couldn't possibly be, because this was a hotel, and breaking into a hotel was a rare occurrence. Then a room mix-up. Or a double booking. Or maybe the bellboy had returned to inform me about my pay-TV options.

Clutching my handbag to my chest, I tiptoed out the living room and toward the closed doors down the hall. A door opened and I bumped into something hard and big. My mouth opened to scream but the sound remained lodged in my throat. And then arms went around me, the scent of shower gel and aftershave wafting over and enveloping me like a sheath.

I looked up at Chase, my blood boiling.

Dressed in nothing but a towel that hung low on his hips and barely managed to hide an inch of his sculpted body, he looked like a beautiful statue that had come alive.

Basically naked.

And within a hand's reach.

"Good to see you, Laurie." He laughed and his arms tightened around my waist, as though to steady me even though I needed no support.

"What are you doing here?" The words came out so thin I cringed. Behind him I glimpsed a spacious bathroom, lined with Carrera marble, and equipped with a whirlpool big enough to host an entire family, and a glass-enclosed shower.

"Obviously, I crash here. Just as per our arrangement."

"But…" I struggled for words, numbed by the absurdity of the situation. Could I throw his ass out even though he had paid for the suite?

Hardly.

Oblivious to my thoughts and obviously misinterpreting my long and hard stare, Chase grinned. "No worries. The bathroom's large enough for two. It even has a whirlpool that will fit both you and me. We'll have to squeeze together a bit, but that won't be a problem. I'll gladly let you sit on my lap."

I looked past his broad and very naked shoulders. The

whirlpool was so huge, you could practically swim in there.

The word "lap" managed to stir something within my core.

"Let go of me." I took a step back, my gaze traveling down his chest to the damp, white fabric that seemed to draw all attention to a generous bulge. I knew I was staring, but for some inexplicable reason my eyes just couldn't look elsewhere.

"You want a close-up?" Chase asked. "Because I'd be more than happy to oblige."

All heat drained from my face.

I stared at him, shaking my head.

Sometimes Chase amazed me with his bluntness, but right now he amazed me with his stupidity. Did he really think that by looking so deliciously sexy or choosing a suite with a whirlpool he'd manage to make me want to sleep with him?

Definitely not.

I wasn't that desperate.

"You're crazy," I whispered. "Just because you're naked, I harbor absolutely no intention of sleeping with you, Chase. I hope you know that."

"Yeah, you told me." He laughed. "It's easy for you to say now. But come tomorrow, you might not feel the same way, which is why I'll stay near you in case you change your mind about our wedding night." He winked. "And then I'll be here, baby, making all your dreams come true, and then some."

He didn't even make a secret out of his inflated ego.

"Crazy." I pointed a finger to my head, annoyed with my monosyllabic answers.

"One day you'll see."

"Dream on." I scowled and took another step back.

Obviously, he was laughing at me, and given the fact that the entire situation was ridiculous, I couldn't blame him. But the knowledge angered me nonetheless. His arrogant comment and his exasperating confidence demanded a comeback…if only my brain functioned well enough that I could think of one. Instead, I turned sharply and headed for the next door, keeping my head high.

Chase laughed behind me. The low, sexy tone both grated on my nerves and sent a tiny shudder through my belly. My hand clasped around the doorknob and I pulled, but the door didn't open. I tried again, then with more fervor.

Why wouldn't the damn thing open?

I could feel him behind me a moment before he leaned over me and whispered in my ear, "You've got to push the right buttons."

His warm breath tickled my neck, sending more shivers through me. He stood so close I could smell his aftershave—the one that always sent my head spinning.

Ever so slowly, he inched forward, his hard abs pressing against my back as he reached for a bolt and slid it open. I could almost feel him through my clothes, as though they had magically melted away. Maybe it was the knowledge that he was half-naked, his lips dangerously close to my ear.

Skin on skin—the sensation was so delicious I marveled at how good it felt and how much I wanted more.

My breath hitched in my throat as he leaned closer, his body melting into me. His hardness rubbed against my lower back as his hand traveled down my chest, settling on my hips. My heart stopped and I forgot to breathe. I closed my eyes, unable to think or move.

"Why are you running?" His voice was deep and…hoarse.

It was a mere question, nothing sexual about it, but his words, mingled with his gentle tone, managed to scare me even more than his immediate proximity and his touch.

"Why are you really here?" I countered with a question of my own, because there was no point in denying the obvious.

"I'm getting married tonight," Chase whispered against my skin. "I'm getting married to a mysterious but very frustrating woman."

I laughed. Oh, I knew all about frustration around him. "That wasn't my question. I meant here, in this room with me."

He let go of my hips and moved back, putting some safe distance between us. I could almost feel his arrogant smile. For the umpteenth time since I'd met him, my blood began to boil.

"It's a suite, meaning there's more than one bedroom. You have yours and I have mine. We'll be neighbors or, if you prefer, roomies, because we share the bathroom and the living room." He pointed to the door on the right. "You'll find my bedroom's next to yours, in case you want to pay me a visit. Any questions?"

I eyed the door to the right, full of mistrust. "What do you mean next to mine?" I asked, confused. "There's just one door to one room."

His lips twitched. "My room has two doors. One through the bathroom and one through yours."

The fluttering sensation in my belly turned into churning conviction.

"Your room's connected with mine?" I asked, and shook my head in disbelief. If I locked the bathroom door and forgot to unlock it, the only way out for Chase would be through my bedroom. And if I wanted to take a shower, he could enter anytime.

"You can't be serious." I turned to regard him, my eyes ablaze with the kind of anger that burned a wicked trail through my entire body. "I said different rooms, which means separate doors, different entries, different everything."

I sounded so ridiculously fraught, it was almost painful to listen to myself, and yet I couldn't stop the sudden wave of desperation washing over me. Chase was everything I dreamed of. But dreaming was one thing and having it in real life was another. He kept challenging me, pushing my limits, forcing me to accept the unacceptable.

I was attracted to him, yes, but I couldn't let him fuck me, because once we passed that threshold I'd enter uncharted territory.

I'd be out of my depth.

Lost.

And he'd hold all the power.

Over my body.

Over my mind.

"Last time I checked there were doors. Quite solid ones, actually." A flicker of amusement lit up his gray-blue eyes. "They have knobs, which means you can open and close them."

I swallowed a few gulps of air to calm myself. "Fine. You can keep the suite. I'll sleep in Jude's."

"It's a single. Not only won't she share, but hotel policy says single rooms are for single occupancy only. Tough luck, beautiful."

Someone knew a lot about hotels.

"I'm getting my own room, Chase," I said, raising my

chin defiantly. "You can't lock me up in here, and you know that."

"That's a tempting outlook, though." His eyes shimmered with danger and humor. "I'd love to lock you up in my bedroom, preferably tied to a bed, and have my wicked ways with you. I'd f—"

Whoa!

"It's not funny," I said, interrupting him before he got me so heated I'd end up begging him to fuck me on the spot.

"You can't avoid me for the rest of your life. May I remind you, we have an agreement, which you agreed to?" Chase crossed his arms over his chest, managing to draw my attention back to his defined muscles and taut skin, as he regarded me coolly.

"Still doesn't mean I have to spend the night in here."

"Suit yourself, sweetheart. But I've got to warn you, they're completely booked. There's a convention in town. Something about..." He paused in mock concentration.

Irritated, I waved my hand. "I don't care. I'll find a solution. I always do. Once I explain the situation, they'll *have* to give me a different room. Or else I'll check into another hotel."

"I'm glad to hear you have such a strong belief in yourself and your persuasion skills." That galling trace of amusement again. "But unless you're a celebrity or can buy out the place, I doubt they'll budge."

Damn, he had a point.

I bit my lip hard as I considered my options.

I could try and risk yet more ridicule because

a.) I wasn't a celebrity, and

b.) I couldn't even afford to pay for one room, let alone the entire hotel.

Or I could take a blow to my pride for the time being and just sleep in the room next to his. How hard could it be?

We wouldn't even have to see each other until the wedding, and then again at checkout tomorrow. That is…if I devised a good plan for this whole roommate thing and stuck to it.

Like who used the bathroom when.

No bedroom visits.

No running around half-naked. And just to make sure he wasn't defying my wishes yet again, I'd listen for any sounds before venturing out to avoid the whole colliding-into-each-other-half-naked-and-drooling-over-his-hard-body situation. If I focused on being very careful and blocked him out of my mind, I wouldn't even know he was here. It shouldn't be that difficult, considering I had avoided hot guys like him before.

Only, I had never met anyone as hot as Chase. Or as willing to let me know just how much I had to fight to keep my legs closed.

"So, what will it be, Laurie?" he asked. "I'm not forcing you to do anything you don't want to. But you can't keep running away from me forever. Sooner or later you'll live with me, anyway. Those last few hours of avoiding me won't change a thing."

"Okay. You win." I smiled sweetly. "But just to be clear. You do not enter my room unless you knock or I open the door to let you in."

"Got it. You want professional and platonic; I'll give you plenty of cool and friendly." He was making fun of me again. Ignoring him, I walked past him into the hall, back to where the bellboy had dropped my baggage. Chase's footsteps echoed behind and I could almost *feel* his irritating grin. The back of my skin prickled from his stare as I grabbed my suitcase, then pulled. It didn't move from the spot. I pulled again, realizing the tiny wheels must have tangled with the thick rug.

Dammit!

As I kept pulling, I could almost see my dignity flying out the window.

"Let me." Chase's hand brushed mine, sending another electric tingle through me. Without waiting for my reply, he lifted the suitcase as though it weighed nothing and carried it down the hall to the first door and opened it, pointing inside.

"This is yours. I took the liberty of choosing the one with the better view. You know, first come and all that." His intense gaze traveled down the front of my shirt and he licked his lips slowly.

Oh, Christ.

Did he have to be so obvious that he wanted me?

"Whatever." I rolled my eyes and pointed at the suitcase. "Just put it down. I'll manage from here."

"As you wish. If you need anything…" As he dropped the suitcase to my feet, his gaze brushed my top again, lingering far longer than was necessary or decent. I grabbed the suitcase and pulled it after me, then slammed the door in Chase's face.

His laughter rang loud and clear, but I didn't care. Whatever game he was playing, I was going to win, no matter what. Even though Chase had the uncanny ability of leaving me in lust and longing, I had one advantage: I had declined myself so often in my life that I had enough practice to say no even if I didn't want to.

Chapter 18

I had barely made it into my room and unzipped my suitcase, filling the wardrobe with my clothes, when a soft knock at the door interrupted me, followed by the door opening.

"What now?" I yelled, and looked up to see Jude standing in the doorway. Her forehead creased in a questioning frown as she settled on my bed and tucked her legs beneath her the way she always did when she harbored no immediate intention of leaving. Her blonde hair swayed around her as she leaned forward, eyes focused on me.

"Don't start," I whispered, referring to Chase's choice of a room: too expensive, too everything for me, not least because it wasn't a real wedding.

She shrugged. "It's not that bad."

"Oh please. He's a nightmare," I whispered. "Can I sleep in your room?" Avoiding her probing gaze, I began to arrange my clothes in the closet.

"Have you seen it?" She snorted. "It's like a mixture between a matchbox and a soda can. Too much wood and metal. This hotel is way overrated."

That was a no, then. I sighed and turned to face her. "Wanna switch?"

"What? Hell no. There's no way I'm sleeping in here."

"Why not?"

"Because"—She threw her hands up in pretend exasperation—"it's your wedding night."

I shrugged. "So?"

"So you deserve the best." She emphasized the last word like it was something naughty. I frowned, not getting her, and then the meaning of her words dawned on me. She wasn't talking about the room; she was talking about Chase.

"This isn't the honeymoon suite." I cringed inwardly at the fact that I felt sort of disappointed at the thought. "Besides, he's sleeping next door. Please switch with me," I begged, whispering in case he could miraculously hear me, which he couldn't, obviously. Given his arrogance, he probably assumed the entire world was talking about him anyway.

"It's *your* wedding," Jude repeated, like that in itself

carried enough weight to justify that she was being a shitty friend by not helping me out. "Besides, it's only one night and you'll be fine. After you get married, Chase will probably hover around the bar until dawn, chatting up girls, and you'll have the entire suite to yourself."

She was probably right, but the thought didn't manage to raise my spirits. If anything, they took a nosedive. I groaned and zipped up my empty suitcase, then dropped it at the bottom of the closet and closed the doors.

"I hope he'll do that," I mumbled through gritted teeth, not meaning a word. Somehow, the idea of Chase hooking up with some random woman was worse than spending the evening arguing with him while fighting off his arrogance the size of a mammoth. Where was he, anyway, and why the heck hadn't he bothered me in—I checked the time on my cell phone—ten minutes?

"You want to grab lunch or something?" I asked.

"Sorry, I'm getting room service. I've got a videoconference call for work, for which I might be late."

I nodded, remembering that she had told me she'd need to fly back early in the morning so she wouldn't miss shooting, but I was thankful for her company and support, even if only for a few hours. After that, I'd be on my own fighting my way through the marriage jungle.

"Thanks for coming. I really appreciate it," I said.

"Don't mention it."

Jude jumped up and placed a sloppy kiss on my cheek, then headed out, calling over her shoulder, "Meet you later to help?" She tilted her head meaningfully toward the plastic-covered gown on my bed.

I nodded again and watched Jude close the door, then dropped on my bed, considering my options.

I *had* to get lunch at some point. Should I venture out or order in? I figured if I stayed in, I'd obsess about the wedding, which was in just a few hours.

In four hours and forty-five minutes, to be exact.

My shoulders slumped and my heartbeat picked up in speed.

But if I left the room, the chance that I might bump into Chase was too high. Even though he had said he'd be gone on a job, I didn't trust him. In the end, I ordered a sandwich and spent the afternoon checking emails and possible job openings in New York City, and sending out my résumé to people who probably wouldn't even glance at it.

A few hours later, I trudged into the bathroom and took a hot shower, then slipped into my seamless underwear.

By six p.m.—with an hour left and no Jude in sight—I could feel the tension in my shoulders. Where the heck was she? I grabbed my phone and called her, only to find that her cell was switched off. She was probably still at work. If she wasn't back anytime soon, I figured I'd have to leave without her.

My mood plummeted when it shouldn't have.

Why did it matter, anyway? It was just a fake wedding. Chase hadn't called to enquire about me. My fake bridesmaid had yet to arrive. And the dress was still wrapped in a plastic bag, seemingly forgotten.

With slow steps, I reached it, my hands itching to touch it as I imagined myself wearing it. And yet I couldn't.

The moment had come—that one special moment I had hoped Jude would share with me. With a sigh, I unzipped the bag and removed the plastic bag carefully, holding my breath as I did so. At first, I noticed that the fabric was different. It was shiny, like the color of a pearl, sparkling translucently the way Chase's eyes had shimmered in the sunlight when he looked at me. My hands brushed gingerly over the soft material for a few seconds before I plucked up my courage and I slipped into it, stepping in front of the mirror.

A smile touched my lips.

It was beautiful.

The skirt fell around me in a perfect, narrow silhouette, emphasizing my bust. Under normal circumstances, that part of my body wouldn't have been my best or favorite feature but, regarding my image in the mirror, even I couldn't deny the extra padding and support gave me a flattering hourglass figure to die for.

The miracles of great tailoring.

But what I liked best about it was the fact that it didn't scream bridal gown—more like an upscale evening dress I could have worn to the opera or a red carpet event. It had all the features of the Vera Wang dress and more. Casey's grandmother had done more than just a fantastic job. I felt like hugging her again and complimenting her skills. If I had the money, I would have asked her to be my personal tailor.

My back turned to the mirror, I admired the fine details of the stitching, then spun around again. Retrieving my mental to-do list, I ticked off all points as I went along. First, I arranged my hair so it'd fall in soft strands around my face, then hastily applied makeup. My hands shook slightly as I arranged a beautiful crown—interlaced wire vines adorned with dainty white blossoms—which Jude insisted I wear in my hair, and applied some perfume.

I stepped back, more nervous than ever. A short glance at the watch confirmed I only had twenty minutes left.

It was time to leave the bathroom in search of my bridesmaid and groom. Stepping out of my room, I noticed how quiet the suite had become. The living room was empty. I squeezed into my high heels and almost slipped on a stray rose petal. Bending to pick it up, I noticed a trail of them and followed it down the hall to the door. I didn't consider Chase might have been the one to think of something so romantic until I saw Jude standing there and she said, "It was all Chase's idea. I told him he was going overboard and that you're not the romantic kind, but he wouldn't listen." She opened the door and inclined her head. "You still doing this?"

Nodding, I left the safety of the suite, wondering for the umpteenth time whether I was making a big mistake.

Too late, Hanson.

Even though it was a pretend marriage, I wouldn't ditch Chase at the altar.

"The dress is gorgeous, by the way," Jude said.

"Thanks," I mumbled. In silence, we rode the elevator down to the lobby and then got into a waiting SUV.

Even though it was still early evening, the street seemed surprisingly devoid of life. I turned my gaze out the window to stare at the dusking sun streaking the sky in orange hues that was mirrored in the countless glass buildings. But even the natural beauty of a setting sun couldn't distract me from my thumping heart and the knowledge of what I was about to do.

"You'll be okay," Jude said, repeating her words from earlier.

I nodded even though the rock in the pit of my stomach was beginning to grow to ominous dimensions.

Chapter 19

The chapel was an inconspicuous building in a residential area in New York City, but even so, it couldn't have been more perfect, with its brown brick stone walls and the decorative white flowers lining up the sidewalk and entrance. As Jude and I stepped out of the SUV and into the candlelit chapel, with the traditional church choir playing in the background, and a professional photographer taking snapshots, tears started to well up. I realized Chase's friend—whoever he was—had done an amazing job finding it and organizing the necessary paperwork in such a short time. I made a mental note to send him a thank-you note, and smiled at Jude with more confidence than I actually felt.

I saw Chase as soon as we entered, and for a second the

world seemed to stop around me when our eyes connected. He was standing at the altar, his sexy, hard body dressed in a tailored tux, his blue eyes shimmering like dark puddles that swallowed up the dim candlelight.

"You look beautiful." Chase stepped forward to place a soft kiss on my cheek, and as he did so his lips almost brushed mine, the gesture instantly cutting off my air supply. I swallowed hard to get rid of the sudden lump in my throat, and pointed at him.

"You don't look so bad, either." My words sounded too low, too alien in my ears.

Chase smiled, and his fingers interlaced with mine. "Ready to yield your single*doom* forever?" He was making fun of me even though I detected no humor in his eyes. No sarcasm in his voice. Poker face all the way.

In spite of my nerves, I found myself smiling. "Did you just say—"

"Sorry, I meant singledom." His gorgeous lips twitched slightly, but his eyes remained glued to me, probing, looking beyond the façade I had worked so hard to build around me. His tailored black suit hugged his athletic body in all the right places, and the white shirt brought out his pale bronze skin. I couldn't decide whether he looked sexier wearing a suit or dressed casually in blue jeans and a snug shirt.

Or maybe nothing at all.

Heat rose up my neck and face. I had almost forgotten

the towel episode from the previous night. That one was by far my favorite. I'd welcome the sight on a daily basis. Not that I would admit that to him. It was bad enough that he knew his tongue on my skin had me blushing, or that his touch left me reeling.

"Laurie?" Chase's brows shot up. "Are you bailing?"

"No. I was just—"

"Staring at me?" His lips twitched again.

"No." I blushed again. "I was trying to figure you out." I rolled my eyes in case my words failed me as I slowly began to wilt under his intense gaze—too dark, too broody.

Come on, Hanson. It's just a man.

Yeah, right, just a man whose teeth were nibbling on my ear.

Could I describe him as just anyone?

Not quite. Because I was about to marry him, and my racing heart wouldn't stop reminding me of his blue eyes shimmering like an ocean in the morning sun, or the sexy, hoarse voice he used in and outside of the bedroom.

"I forgot to give you this." Chase grasped a bouquet of pink roses and ivory calla lilies from a wooden bench and pressed it into my hand.

"They're beautiful." I lifted the bouquet to my face and inhaled the sweet scent of lilies, wondering how he could have possibly known what my favorite flowers were? He'd even got the color right.

"They're beautiful."

"Just like you," Chase said. For a few moments we just gazed at each other, caught up in the moment.

Caught up in whatever was between us.

"I'm sorry this place isn't anything special," he added. "But at least it'll look real."

Real.

A tiny pang of disappointment shot through me. Of course he would remember why we were really here.

What had I been thinking? That he had forgotten about our agreement and plans?

I scanned the tiny chapel. What the heck was he talking about? The place, with its Victorian theme and the few rows of white wooden benches decorated with cream ribbons and more roses, was stunning. Maybe it didn't scream New York elegance. But it wasn't exactly Las Vegas with Elvis memorabilia and tacky décor. Then again, being a West Coast girl, what did I know about New York?

Somewhere a door opened, and people started to spill in, taking their seats, some of them even waving at us.

"Who are they?" I asked, stunned.

"Our fake audience." Chase smiled, obviously amused, as the photographer snapped away. And then the wedding officiant entered and the ceremony began.

***

The whole thing was over in less than twenty minutes. From the moment Chase and I confirmed the authenticity of our documents, to the hasty 'I do' and the signing of the papers, it all passed in a surreal blur. At some point I thought I heard Jude sighing behind me, but I didn't look because I was both overwhelmed and mesmerized, floating in a dreamlike state of disbelief. Chase pulled out a wedding ring and slipped it onto my finger, then demanded that I do the same. The idea that we might need wedding rings hadn't even occurred to me, but he seemed to have thought of everything. Eventually, the officiant pronounced us husband and wife, and before I could blink, Chase kissed me in front of Jude and the paid audience.

Kissed me as if it was real.

His lips—soft and velvety—probed mine, demanding that I play along. And I did willingly, my stomach fluttering as he explored my mouth. I would have continued, savoring him right there and then, if only he hadn't stopped.

My head spun as we left the chapel strangely elated.

The moment we opened the door, I closed my eyes, enjoying the soft light of the moon on my skin. I inhaled deeply, welcoming the strange, happy thoughts and my new life.

I had signed the papers. I had taken his name.

Laurie Wright.

I still couldn't believe that I was a married woman.

Chase was now my husband.

He might be just an actor I had hired, but maybe…

No, stop, Laurie.

I took another deep breath and let Chase's fingers intertwine with mine.

"Let's go," he whispered.

"Drinks are on me," Jude proclaimed as soon as we had taken our seats in the waiting SUV that would take us back to the hotel.

"Sure." I peered at Chase from the corner of my eye. His face was turned away from us. In the dim evening light falling in through the windows, I couldn't read his expression, but the impatient tapping of his fingers on his thigh didn't escape my attention. I couldn't blame him. As much as I needed a drink, I'd have rather spent some alone time with him.

"Hey, you in?" Jude elbowed him jokingly.

Chase turned, and in that instant I caught a flicker in his eyes—something dark and hard. And then his eyes turned on me and the flicker disappeared, making room for warmth, and not just a flame, but a whole wildfire of it.

Holy dang.

It was a flicker of desire, like a passion running deep.

He was stunning, now more than ever. Darkness suited him. It brought out the mysterious side to him; the one I had glimpsed on various occasions; the one that had kept my thoughts occupied, tied by invisible chains. To me he was an enigma, just like the night around us.

A warm tingle ran through my abdomen and gathered in the most secret spot of my core. I was attracted to him on a purely sexual level, raw hormones and all. That in itself was worrisome enough. But the fact that I seemed to melt from the inside at the mere twitch of his lips or at a glance from those gray-blue eyes was terrifying.

Never in my life had I felt that way about anybody.

Chase smiled and I smiled back shyly, eager to express my gratitude in some way. After all, he had done me a favor without expecting much in return.

If you call your body 'nothing.'

"Laurie?" His brows shot up, amused. "Do you have anything lined up for tonight?"

Dammit.

There was that double meaning again. My cheeks began to burn, which apparently had become my natural reaction whenever Chase was around. Not only was he out of this world in the looks department, he was also one of those lucky specimens gifted with the uncanny ability to sense other people's emotional undercurrents, specifically those of the sexual kind. Either that, or I was a sad, open book to him. Fool that I was, I liked to think that the latter wasn't the case.

I raised my chin and peered straight into his eyes, holding his gaze daringly. "No. Just drinks."

He chuckled and a flicker of determination appeared in his eyes. I could almost hear the 'we'll see about that part' in his thoughts.

The arrogance!

Chase began to ask questions about Jude's job. What she did; how she liked it; all the while gazing at me. Irritated, I tuned out and focused on New York's City's skyline flitting outside the window.

Eventually the SUV stopped in front of our hotel to let us exit, and I excused myself to change into something more suitable while Chase and Jude waited in the bar area. I placed my flower bouquet in a crystal vase and had barely slipped into a demure black cocktail dress when the door slammed and a low, sultry laugh drifted over from the hall, disturbing the silence that had barely settled around my mind. I pressed my back against the door and strained to listen.

It was definitely Jude's tinkling laughter in our suite's living room. A male voice chuckled and I realized it was Chase. They were having fun. An irrational pang of jealousy hit me in the pit of my stomach, even though I knew my best friend would never flirt with him. She had always been loyal and true to me.

But Chase?

Why was the thought of him having fun with another woman making me jealous? Or worse yet, how come the image of him being with someone else other than me made me feel hurt?

I had known Chase for less than three weeks, during which we had become friends. Sure, we had fun and had gone further than I initially anticipated, but it wasn't possible that I was developing feelings for him, was it? The thought was improbable and yet so scary I gasped for air. Being attracted to him was one thing, but falling in love with my fake husband was another.

I had no claims on him and yet my heart seemed to think otherwise, as though the fact that we were legally married somehow justified the most ridiculous of reactions: a longing to possess him, mind, body, and soul.

I had to get a grip. If I didn't soon, I'd have to find a way to get away from him before I fell too hard.

Another chuckle, then a loud laugh, and my jealousy flared up again.

I straightened my dress and opened the door with a forced smile on my lips.

"Hi." My gaze scanned their faces for clues in a desperate attempt to figure out what was going on.

Chase ambled over and placed a possessive arm around my waist. "We were talking about you."

Oh, God.

"Were you?" I rewarded him with a bright, easygoing smile. If I kept this up I figured I might just fool not only them but also myself.

"Jude was telling me stories about how you got rid of some of her dates over the years. Seems like you're a natural at clearing the perimeter."

Double *oh, God.*

Why did I sound like a complete loser with no love life? Granted, it wasn't far from the truth, but did she *have* to tell Chase?

"Like the one time that guy kept calling and you claimed I was in hospital," Jude said, oblivious to my mortified state of mind. "He wouldn't stop stalking, so you had to tell him you once escaped from a mental hospital. He got so freaked out, I never saw him again. Hilarious."

She fell into another fit of laughter, and Chase chuckled, his grip around my waist tightening. My humiliation was increasing by the second. I had to divert everyone's attention from me, and fast, before Jude started to show him snapshots of us on her cell phone and Chase realized he had made a big mistake by marrying me.

There was only one way to divert Jude's attention to less mortifying territory.

"Hilarious." I faked a laugh. "Didn't you say something about drinks?" I wriggled out of Chase's arms and grabbed my purse from the coffee table. "So where's the party at?"

Chapter 20

The two margaritas combined with the fast, pounding music of the club and steady stream of New Yorkers had made my head more than a little fuzzy. At some point my vision had blurred and all voices seemed to carry a slight drawl, like they were shouting through a long tunnel and the sound came out all distorted.

Closing my eyes for a moment, I took a deep breath and then exhaled slowly, wondering why I wasn't in my extravagant suite, tucked into bed, watching soap operas on the oversized television set. Then I remembered the main two reasons, one being Jude's inevitable tendency to recall the most embarrassing details of our lives. And the second being—

Chase.

Oh, God. Chase.

For the last hours he'd kept finding the most ridiculous reasons to touch me. Like when he had claimed to need to make a phone call outside the club and his lips *accidentally* brushed my earlobe when he leaned into me to communicate his need to make said phone call.

I figured excusing myself was out of the question, because he'd probably follow me to ask how I was doing. Then he'd pretend to want to give me a goodnight kiss. I'd inhale his manly aftershave and before I knew it I might just have a few things to regret the following morning.

I had to stall as long as I could, and if that involved downing a few margaritas in the process then so be it.

"Another one?" Jude pointed at my empty glass, grinning.

I nodded hesitantly and she hurried over to the bar area to get our order, then returned with two glasses and left again to hit the dance floor. Chase hadn't returned from his important phone call, so I grabbed my glass out of sheer boredom and took a sip, then another, and before I realized it, it was empty again.

My head began to spin faster, and not in a good way. I groaned and scrambled out of my chair, realizing my legs weren't faring much better.

Dammit.

What was it with me and my inability to party like most people my age?

Was there some secret about drinking that no one had revealed to me, or did I inherit some gene that made me respond to the slightest hint of alcohol?

I took a few steps, but the room started to spin.

"Need help?"

Before I knew it Chase's arm was around my waist again and I found myself pressed hard against his chest. My heart—the fool that it was—skipped a few beats, and an unnatural warmness crept up between my legs.

Oh my God, I was really, embarrassingly drunk.

"I don't need help." I pushed him away, but it might only have happened in my mind, because I could feel his lips nestling against my neck.

Hot, sexy breath.

"I don't doubt that, but it would be irresponsible of me if I left you like this," Chase said.

"Jude can help me to my room."

"She already left."

What?

"Come on, Laurie. I'll get you into bed before you pass out," Chase said against my ear, and coincidently his lips found my earlobe again, setting my nerve endings on fire.

Bed.

I liked that word a lot.

A strong jolt rattled my core, and a pull built inside, urging me to still it. Usually I would have done so myself, taking care of my needs. But this time my body longed for someone else's touch.

No, not someone's touch.

Chase's.

I realized it had done so ever since I met him.

The thought of being so weak for him made me cringe inwardly.

I had thought that by numbing my feelings with alcohol, I'd escape my obsession with him, but apparently my desire for him wasn't going to play along.

I craved him, unable to stifle the sudden wish of getting a whole lot closer to him than before.

As if sensing my naughty thoughts, Chase's hands wrapped around me. "It's getting late."

"I can't leave yet," I protested, only my voice sounded way more clear in my mind than when it left my mouth. As though to prove my point, my hand wrapped around Jude's glass. Chase stopped it in midair.

"You've had enough, Laurie." Chase's voice was low but determined.

He was right, of course, but in a brief moment of sudden lucidness my need to protest against a man telling me what to do won the war against my better judgment.

"You're not stopping me, sir." I giggled and lifted the

glass to my lips to take a gulp. The sickeningly sweet liquid traveled down my throat and left a repulsive aftertaste in my mouth.

I wasn't a fan of alcohol, but more so I wasn't a fan of dominating men.

I had had my fair share with Clint.

"That's it. You're my wife, and I say you're going home before you blame me for the mother of hangovers tomorrow morning." Chase snapped the glass out of my hand and put it on the table. His grip released my waist and tightened around my upper arm as he guided me out of the bar. It was a bad move, and somewhere inside my mind countless alarm bells went off all at once, urging me to call Jude.

But I didn't dare, because, in my drunken state, everything became a blur and I realized I needed a bed more than I needed to demonstrate my independence.

"Fine." I trudged in front of him, relishing the touch of his hand on my body as we stepped into a taxi. Within half an hour, we were back at the hotel, his hand guiding me through the huge revolving doors, past the lobby, to the second bank of elevators.

So close he smelled amazing, like sun, earth and rain— all intermingled in one heady fragrance. Did he taste as good as he smelled?

"I guess you'll have to find that out yourself," he said,

and pressed a button.

"What?" I asked, confused.

"If I taste as good." He grinned.

I stared at him, shell-shocked.

Holy shit.

Did I really say that out loud?

His smile vanished as he eyed me, worried. "That was a joke, Laurie. I know you don't mean what you say."

"But what if I do?" I blurted out before I could stop myself.

Stunned silence.

What the fuck was wrong with me?

I should never have drunk so much.

"You want me?" he asked at last.

"Yes." I nodded with more passion than I wanted.

"Laurie." He sighed. "I told you I'll help you out, but I don't want you to feel obliged to repay me that way just because we signed the papers."

"No, I know that, and I still want you," I whispered. "I want you to be my first."

Oh my God, shoot me!

I should never have told myself to stay away from him, because now I really wanted him, my body urging me to do the opposite. It was proof that my mind had no control over my desires. Chase had become a thrill; the forbidden fruit I couldn't taste but couldn't resist.

Cocking his head to the side, he frowned. "You're drunk. We all say things we don't mean when we're drunk."

"Obviously not so drunk as to not know who you are."

He laughed briefly. "It's a relief you recognize your husband." He grew quiet again as his hand moved to his pocket. "I like you, and I'll admit I really want you, too, but there's no way in hell I'm taking advantage of you in this state."

"Right." I faked a careless shrug, suddenly feeling silly. "It was just a stupid idea."

"Yeah, it was," he agreed, sounding doubtful. "It would have been a mistake."

"A big mistake," I agreed.

Turning away, I watched the digits above the elevator climbing steadily upward. Fifteen. Sixteen. Seventeen. Upward they went, lighting up whenever they passed a floor. At last they stopped at thirty.

Thirty.

I had been supposed to take the interview on the thirtieth floor in the LiveInvent building. The elevator stopped at the twenty-ninth floor.

The word echoed at the back of my mind. A layer of sweat covered my back, and my heart raced. The incident had taken place more than three months ago, when I watched an entire floor collapse. Three months haunted by memories of being stuck in a lift with a stranger. Three months of guilt that I had done nothing to save him. Three months of being reminded that I almost died.

Was he dead or alive?

That question constantly frequented my thoughts. My heart lurched again, and slowly the spinning sensation started.

Breathe in, breathe out.

"Are you okay?" Chase's voice sounded like it came through a tunnel.

I nodded unconvincingly.

The digits climbed down again. The bell chimed when the elevator doors opened, but I didn't move.

One wrong step—that was all it took.

The whole interview had been a mistake.

I never should have gone, because if it weren't for me, if I hadn't been inside, the stranger would have been rescued instead of me.

"You don't look okay. Do you want to take the stairs?" Chase said.

I turned to him, feeling faint. "I'm fine."

My voice was shaking.

His arms engulfed me, and he started to rub my back. Just like the stranger had done in the elevator.

"You're hyperventilating, Laurie."

Oh my God. Was it starting again?

"Breathe, Laurie. You need to breathe."

Even his voice sounded like Mystery Guy. I closed my eyes, overcome by faintness as the memories started rolling before my eyes. It was the stupid alcohol wreaking havoc on my body and mind, opening my barriers, letting the memories I had tried to lock away flood back in.

"You sound like him," I whispered.

"Like who?"

He was so much like him, and yet I couldn't tell Chase without sounding crazy.

"I'm sorry. I can't." And then I started to run.

Chapter 21

Chase found me outside the revolving doors, my arms crossed over my chest as I took long, deep, calming breaths.

Gently, he turned me to him. "I'm sorry. I should never have asked. It was not my business and—"

"No." I shook my head. "I'm the one who needs to apologize. I should never have drunk so much. Alcohol messes with my head." I took in the concern etched into his features, wondering whether I should share with him the events of that fateful day. "When I saw the digits, I freaked out. It reminded me too much of…" I trailed off, my guilt consuming me again.

"Do you want to talk it?"

"No." I shook my head again. "No, I can't." I looked at him again in the hope he'd forgive me. In the hope one day

I'd forgive myself. "Can you we please forget what just happened? It's stupid, and I'm ruining our evening."

He took a long breath, his arms dropping to the side in what I assumed was disappointment. "Sure."

For a few seconds we stood there until Chase broke the awkward silence. "See them?" He pointed to a couple stepping out of a limousine. A woman in her thirties, dressed in a beautiful bridal gown, was snapping at her newlywed husband, who could barely stand on his feet.

Faint words carried over. "Why didn't you marry her, then? I leave you for one second, one frigging second, and you're already all over the fucking bridesmaid."

"That could have been us." Chase smiled at me. "My point is things could be much worse. Being afraid of an elevator or of darkness is human. We all have our own fears and demons to deal with, but I want you to know that I'm here for you."

"I'm not afraid of elevators," I said matter-of-factly. I didn't know what came over me, but I grabbed his hand and began to pull him behind me, as though to prove a point. "Come on. We don't have all night."

The elevator doors opened.

Chase followed me inside willingly. "You sure you want to—"

I nodded, feeling way too bold.

As soon as the doors of the elevator closed us in, I

pressed myself against Chase's body and nuzzled my mouth against his neck to place a kiss on his soft skin.

He didn't resist.

The stubble on his chin grazed my cheek as his mouth found mine, and our tongues met in a sensual tangle. His lips were soft and tender, demanding without being aggressive, his tongue playing with mine.

His palm moved down the front of my dress, grazed my breasts, and settled on the small of my back with possessive pressure.

He wanted me—I had figured that one out a while ago, but now I could feel it in the growing tightness in his pants. His warm breath caressed my face. His hands stroked my back.

I clasped my hands at the back of his neck and pulled him closer. His hard length brushed my body, demanding my immediate attention. My legs began to tremble, and I moaned against his open mouth, unsure whether to continue or pull back. Luckily, the elevator doors opened with a soft whir and Chase peeled himself from me, his face flushed with excitement as we stumbled out into the vestibule. He didn't glance at me while retrieving his entry card from his pocket and swiping it.

"We're here," I said, stating the obvious. My tone reflected the slight disappointment inside my mind.

Ignoring my needless remark, Chase let us in and closed

the door behind us. I almost expected him to press me against the wall and resume our groping session, but his back remained turned on me, his shoulders surprisingly tense, as though, like me, he was fighting to make the right decision.

"It's fine." I pressed my fingertips against his shoulder blade and trailed them down his back slowly. Even through his shirt his muscles felt hard and strong. I bit my lip as I pondered my options. Maybe it was the alcohol or my earlier freak-out incident, but something had ignited inside me and I was eager to find out where it would lead me. Obviously, I wasn't going to go all the way—maybe just a few more kisses to get him out of my system. And then I'd go to bed satisfied.

"I'm not taking advantage of a woman in your state," Chase said hoarsely without looking at me.

"And what state is that?"

"You're drunk." He turned to face me, his expression unreadable, but his eyes were a grim blue, like a stormy afternoon.

"I'm not that drunk," I whispered.

Chase shook his head and grabbed my hand, leading me into my bedroom. "Good night, Laurie."

"What about you?"

"I'm calling it an early night."

He slammed the door. I stared at the empty space he

had just occupied. I should have been thankful for his self-control, but for some inexplicable reason I found myself disappointed at his change of tone. For the first time in my life I had actually invited a man to do more than just talk and he was blowing me off.

"Damn you," I muttered, and texted Jude that I was going to bed, then stormed into the bathroom and took a long shower that cleared some of the fog inside my mind. It was almost midnight when I'd finished with my usual evening routine, and I switched off the lights and went to bed, unable to sleep for a long time knowing that Chase was sleeping next door.

Damn the hot guy.

Chapter 22

I awoke to the faint sound of footsteps outside my door. The room was bathed in darkness. I sat up straight and listened for more sounds. My head felt surprisingly alert as I threw a glance at my phone on the bedside table. It was shortly before four a.m. Everything seemed quiet again, and yet I couldn't shake off the eerie feeling that someone was outside my door. I could almost feel their presence. It had to be Chase, because no one else had access to our suite, and yet my heartbeat spiked and a faint sense of fear threatened to throttle me.

Carefully I got up and tiptoed to the door, then pressed my ear against it. When nothing stirred, I opened the door and peered into the darkness. Apart from the faint silhouettes of the furniture, the corridor was empty.

"Chase?" I whispered, even though I didn't expect him to answer. I waited for a moment or two before realizing my sleepiness had deserted me, and my heartbeat hadn't noticeably slowed down. Whatever I heard, it wasn't Chase, or he would have replied. Straining my ears, I listened for more sounds, but they never came.

In a bold moment of confidence, I headed for Chase's room and let myself in, then stopped in the doorway, realizing what I had just done. Whatever had woken me had scared me a little, but not to the extent that it might serve as an excuse to shack up with Chase for the night. I turned around to leave again but Chase's voice carried over from the oversized bed.

"Laurie?"

Could I pretend it wasn't me? Maybe I could lie that I had heard him talking in his sleep and had hurried over, worried. Undecided as I was, I stood frozen to the spot. Chase sat up, and the soft light falling through the open curtains illuminated his body in a slow dance of light and shadows.

He was naked.

Oh, come on.

My heart began to beat just a little bit harder, and my mouth went dry at the image of defined muscles and dark bed hair.

"What's up? You had a bad dream?" Chase asked, his

voice deep and sleep-drunken, but sexy as hell as he rubbed the sleep from his eyes.

Dammit, that should have been my line. I bit my lip hard and cleared my throat. "No. I thought I heard something, but it was nothing."

My excuse sounded so unconvincing, even I had trouble believing it.

"Sorry. I shouldn't have come here." I turned my back to open the door, but his voice stopped me.

"Wait."

I turned back to him, feeling the heat creeping into my face.

"You sound scared." To my chagrin, Chase stood and walked over to me in all his naked glory. From head to toe. All hard muscles and pale skin that seemed to invite my fingers to graze my nails over every tempting inch of him.

In the middle of the night, bathed in the weak light of the moon, his body seemed as lithe as a predator's, his stride just as a dangerous.

I fought hard to keep my gaze occupied on anything but his lower abdomen and maleness. He wrapped his arm around my shoulder and led me to the bed, urging me to sit. "Want a glass of water?"

I shook my head even though I figured he might not be able to see it in the dark. He lay down beside me and crossed his ankles, patting the space next to him. I followed his silent invitation with apprehension, leaving some distance between us.

"You can relax," Chase said softly. "I'm not doing anything you don't want to."

But that was the problem...I wanted him to do something to still the sudden throbbing sensation in my private parts. Gingerly I crossed my ankles and pressed my thighs together, which only managed to intensify the sensation.

Oh, God.

His body smelled so inviting of aftershave and warmth and—

Sex.

The word hit my mind with such an intensity I almost jumped up and dashed for the door. Only, my legs didn't seem to want to follow my brain's command. I bit my lip hard and inched just a little bit closer to him. As though sensing my emotional turmoil, Chase squeezed his arm under my shoulder and pulled me up until my head rested on his chest. The gesture was probably supposed to infuse a sense of calm into me, but it only managed to raise my awareness of his naked body.

So perfect. So close. So available.

Damn it.

Slowly I trailed my fingers up his abdomen, my fingertips barely touching his taut skin and hard muscles.

Chase drew in his breath sharply, and for a moment his body tensed under my touch. In the darkness his gaze found mine with an intensity that rendered me unable to breathe. And in that moment I knew I was ready.

"Don't start something you cannot finish, Laurie," Chase said hoarsely.

Jutting my chin out, I increased my pressure as my fingertips grazed up and down his chest, coming dangerously close to the one part I had not dared to look at yet. His breathing came labored, but if my touch tortured him he made no move to stop me. In the darkness surrounding us I smiled as I realized I liked this new development in our relationship, whatever that entailed.

I wanted him. I wanted him so badly it hurt. To my surprise, I realized my body knew exactly how to react to him.

"Laurie." Chase's voice was a mere whisper, but the air charged with something. Before I knew it, he turned, his body leaning over me. Underneath him, I felt hot. Ready. His lips crushed mine, his tongue invading my mouth forcefully, sending my abdomen on fire. I spread my legs slightly to accommodate his weight and ran my fingers across his back, pulling him closer.

Chase moaned into my mouth and his hand began to roam over my body, lifting my nightshirt to expose my breasts, then to remove my panties. His kisses felt as smooth as water falling down on me, covering each inch of my neck and breasts.

A strangled sound caught in my throat as his hands forced my thighs apart and he settled between them, his mouth eager to touch me in the one secret place no man but him had ever touched.

I squirmed against his open mouth, unsure whether to push him away or give in to the hot sensations gathering deep within my core. And then his finger dipped into me, gently at first, then with more fervor, and I knew I was lost. It couldn't stop this even if I wanted to. It felt too good to have him on me. Inside me. Soothing the need he seemed to awaken like no other.

My back arched and my hips lifted slightly against his slow thrusts so he could reach deeper within me.

"Chase." My voice quivered, just like my body.

"Lean back," he commanded. "Don't fight this."

Even if I knew how, I wasn't going to.

Following his command, I relaxed against the pillows and let him take control—the kind of control I didn't give him the last time.

I promised myself that I'd go through with it. No turning back now.

Chase and I were married, and even if it wasn't real, I wanted him to be my first. It felt right.

His tongue circled my clitoris a few times and then he

began to suckle while his finger thrust deep inside me. I cried out as the room began to spin.

"Chase." My fingers clenched into the bed sheets, and with his name on my lips I fell hard into a dark abyss of pleasure, rootless in a sea of lost reason.

"Dammit. You're hot," Chase whispered. But I couldn't respond. I could barely comprehend the meaning of his words because my world came crashing down on me. Slow waves of pulsating heat gathered between my legs, intensifying with each flick of his tongue.

My breathing came loud and fast, my pulse hammering in my ears.

He wasn't just good. He had the most talented tongue I'd ever met. His finger, slow but steady, did unimaginable things to me. Things I never thought could feel so great. If just one finger was great, what would it feel like to have him inside me?

"Give me just one night so I can forget you," I thought I heard him whisper.

Forget me?

What the hell was that supposed to mean? Or maybe he meant so he wouldn't forget me. The question burned bright in my mind for a second and then it was gone, lost in the throes of heat crashing through my abdomen. I closed my eyes to relish it, realizing just how magnificent it was, his words lost inside my mind.

My body—now wet and trembling—was like an open pool, and then I felt my orgasm coming.

"Chase," I whispered, trying to close my thighs, but he stopped me.

"Don't come." That was all he said.

As if I had any control over my body.

From the periphery of my mind, I felt Chase removing himself from me. Something rustled in the silence and then his body was on top of me again. His mouth found mine in a deliciously slow kiss. For a second I felt panic and the need to protest, to tell him that I wasn't ready for more, that this was all I could handle for the time being. Only, my body seemed to harbor other intentions. It wanted him so much.

Chase had ignited a fire inside me that I knew only he could still.

Another flicker of need pulsed between my legs. It was painful, and desperate. I lifted my hips, unconsciously begging for the friction only he knew how to provide.

"Are you sure you want this?" he asked.

I was, more than ever. Chase had been wonderful to me, and even if our relationship wasn't real, I trusted him enough not to hurt me.

A shuddering sigh escaped my lips.

"I am," I whispered.

Chase settled between my legs, one hand lifting my ass,

the other holding his weight. I could feel his hard erection pulsing against my entrance. My body tensed, but inside I could feel the tremors, and before I could think, he pushed slowly inside me, gently, then stopped. A sudden sense of discomfort ran through my abdomen. Not entirely painful, just strange. I had used my fingers before to masturbate, but this sensation was different—too filling, too stretching—and I wasn't sure that I liked how it felt.

A piece of Chase inside me felt like an invasion of my body.

"Don't move," he whispered in my ear, his voice slightly strained. "You'll get used to it." His muscles began to tremble, and I realized his skin was slick with a thin layer of sweat. From the effort? From self-control? I had no idea. I hoped it wasn't discomfort.

"Are you okay?" I whispered back.

"You're asking *me*?" He chuckled, and, in spite of my nerves, I found myself smiling. "Never felt better. You're just a little bit tight, and it's driving me crazy."

"Oh." I wet my lips when a question came to me. "Does it hurt?"

"Not me, no." He laughed again. "Does it hurt?"

"No," I answered honestly. "It's just…strange."

"It will change." He moved slowly, the motion sending his erection deeper into me. He settled his weight on one elbow, and his other hand moved to my clit. "Now I need you to relax. Okay? Relax, Laurie."

I looked up into his eyes that seemed to swallow up the darkness, wondering whether that was it—the one thing everyone seemed to rave about. It sure didn't feel worth all the hype.

His fingers began to stroke my clit as he moved inside me in slow, deep thrusts. A thin layer of sweat covered my back as the sensation between my legs changed, and a strong longing took its place, demanding more. My hips rolled against him naturally, slowly drawing his erection deeper, like it belonged there. Like it always had.

Chase's sudden moan echoed in my ears, strangely amplified. Knowing I was the object of his desire and the cause of his pleasure, a rush of elation ran through me.

I had no idea that his sexy sounds and his movements could be such a turn-on. His fingers, his erection, his hot breath—everything about him seemed to make me want him even more.

"Is this better?" Chase whispered.

I nodded, and he lifted my legs in response. His erection slipped fully into me, making me gasp from the sudden tension building inside. Chase began to move faster, tentatively at first, then with a firm precision, each thrust entering me deeper, each thrust bringing a new wave of sensations with it.

Burning, all-consuming heat that rendered me unable to

move or think, torturing me until I was ready to beg him to stop because I could take it no more. My heartbeat hammered so hard against my chest, I thought I might just pass out. The room began to swirl again as the intensity of his thrusts changed from fast to slow and deep, hitting a spot within me I never knew existed.

My hands grabbed the sheets for support. I felt if I didn't hold on to them, I might just float away.

"That's it, baby." Chase's deep voice echoed in my ear, urging me to succumb to whatever he was about to give me. The first tremor took me by surprise. The next one rattled my body and sent my senses careening. My fingers clenched into his shoulders as my core unraveled around him. Chase shuddered above me, his last moan prolonging my own pleasure.

And then it was over.

Too quickly. Too fast. And I couldn't avoid the strange nostalgia washing over me, until Chase kissed me and pulled me to his chest. I closed my eyes and gave in to the sudden need to sleep, his words no longer penetrating the wall of exhaustion settling around my mind.

Epilogue

I woke up with a gasp, my brain fighting with the demons occupying my dreams as my eyes adjusted to the light seeping through the drawn curtains. Chase had been in them. And my mother. Somewhere, in the periphery of my vision, I had thought I saw Clint and Shannon, their smiles reserved but wicked, like they knew something I didn't. It had made me angry, not because they were laughing, but because they knew something I didn't.

I took a deep breath and let it out slowly, not yet ready to look at the other side of the bed.

A turning point in my life.

Breathe in, breathe out.

We had done it. And now I was Mrs. Chase Wright. Granted, we hadn't married out of love but it still counted.

Married was married, be it out of love or out of necessity.

Breathe in, hold it, and then breathe out.

But the wedding wasn't even the biggest and most shocking part. I had slept with him and it had been more amazing than I ever envisioned. Strange but amazing nonetheless.

As the air whooshed out of my lungs, I turned to look at the man sleeping on the other side of the bed. In the morning light, Chase was so beautiful I couldn't help but stare, praying in my thoughts that he wouldn't wake and catch me. Because, I knew, if he did I still couldn't pry my eyes off him. His torso was turned away from me, which gave me enough privacy to admire his half naked body.

His features were relaxed, the dark lashes casting shadows across his perfect skin. The thin covers barely hid the perfection of his sculpted chest and abdomen. My gaze lingered on the clearly defined bulge beneath the sheet and my breath hitched in my throat from shame. I had seen naked men before, on television, in magazines and commercials. But none of them had had this effect on me. None of them had made me want to trail my fingertips down his body. Or to sleep with them even though my core felt sore and my body depleted of energy.

My shameful brain began to conjure vivid pictures of last night's events before my eyes and a soft tingle gathered in my breasts. My nipples hardened, begging for Chase's touch. As if he could sense my increasing arousal, Chase stirred but didn't wake.

Oh, God.

I had to get away before he woke up and realized I was getting ready for round two. Whatever I experienced that night with Chase, I wanted it again. I wanted to take charge. I wanted to learn more, but first I had to spruce up, because there was no way in hell I would let a sexy man like him see me naked, all sweaty from last night's action between the sheets, and without make-up.

Gingerly I got out of his bed and pulled my crumpled nightdress over my head, then tiptoed out of the room and closed the door behind me. The hall was bathed in bright, glorious light, reflecting the way I felt inside.

I had almost reached the door to my bedroom to grab my make-up bag when a phone rang. It took me barely a second to spy it on the hardwood floor under the table in the hallway, where I must have dropped it too drunk to notice.

It was most certainly Jude calling.

I squatted quickly to pick it up and pressed it to my ear without checking the caller ID.

I got the chance to answer because a male voice beat me to it.

"You need to get back to me," he barked down the line. "I swear if you lose more money, the deal's gone. Do you hear me? It'll be gone, so you'd better get your ass moving and do what we talked about. You'd better not fuck this up."

The words were harsh—like whiplashes against my bare soul.

I opened my mouth to explain that he had dialed the wrong number when tires screeched, followed by the sound of scraping metal and a crash, ending in a string of cuss words.

"I got to go, bro," the voice said. "The stupid fucker can't drive worth shit. And before I forget, the folder's in the top left drawer of the coffee table beneath the blue painting. Get your fucking shit together or we'll have a real problem on our hands."

He hung up—just like that.

Confused, I stood frozen to the spot, unable to make any sense of the bizarre conversation.

What a creep.

I swiped at the screen to block his number when I was prompted for the password. I frowned.

It was then that I noticed the cell phone was a sleek little iPhone, all shiny and new—probably the newest gadget on the market. Except for the color black, it looked nothing like the second hand phone I bought after my handbag was stolen.

It had to be Chase's cell.

Oh, shit. I didn't want him to think I might be snooping through his stuff.

I peered at Chase's bedroom door out of fear that he might have caught me in the act.

Except for the loud drumming of my heart, everything remained silent.

Letting out a shaky breath to compose myself, I placed the cell phone on the table.

"Don't, Laurie. Just drop it," I murmured to myself. They were supposed to be words of inspiration as I headed for my room.

The curtains were closed, the bed in its previous, dishevelled state. I pulled the curtains aside.

Would Chase know that I had taken his call?

Most likely.

Maybe he won't look. And you can pretend you didn't hear anything.

I'd deal with a confrontation when it happened.

But, for some reason, the call just wouldn't stop pestering me in my mind.

There had been something about the voice—an urgency in the brisk tone, some kind of control it exerted—that worried me.

Suddenly, I felt anxious for Chase. He had been eager to help me, and in all that time, I never really asked questions about his life. For all I knew, he could be drowning in debt.

Or maybe he was addicted to drugs—though, from the looks of his place, I doubted it. He seemed to have his life figured out, or maybe I wanted to see him that way.

There was a real possibility that he was involved with a bad crowd.

Fuck it, Laurie.

My imagination was running wild again—and not in a good way.

The caller must have dialed the wrong number because there was no blue painting in the executive suite.

Or was there?

My heart began to flutter hard against the current of nervous energy engulfing me. I slowed down as new thoughts began to permeate my mind.

It had been in the middle of the night that I heard steps. I had placed them outside my bedroom, in the hall, near the entrance. Was it possible that a visitor had entered to leave the folder?

My mind began to reel at the possibility. Before I knew what came over me, I retraced my steps to the living room and stopped in the doorway. My gaze fell on the painting above the coffee table.

It wasn't blue, per se.

However, the sky and the blue clothes of a pale woman were prevalent enough to catch my attention. Could it be it?

I dashed for it, for some reason afraid that Chase might

catch me if I didn't hurry, but there was no movement, no one to stop me.

I stopped right in front of it. Above the painting, the inscription read 'The Sacrifice of Polyxena.'

But it wasn't the painting or the title that persuaded me to pull open the drawer. I just had to know, even though I expected to find nothing.

The drawer was stuck halfway so I tugged harder, without much success.

I squeezed my arm inside to check the back, and my fingertips brushed something coarse.

The folder was there.

"Holy shit," I whispered.

A rush of excitement flooded me but stopped abruptly, replaced by guilt. I clapped my hand in front of the mouth, thinking.

What are you doing, Laurie?

Technically, we were married, but Chase and I hadn't defined our relationship status just yet. Whatever Chase was doing was his business, and yet, somewhere, somehow deep down, I couldn't help but wonder what sort of trouble he was in. Maybe I could help him. I shouldn't have listened to the guy on the phone because now I was curious.

Shit.

I should never have picked up the phone in the first place.

Shouldn't even have touched it.

But I did, and now what?

Guilt gnawed at me for wanting to find out everything about Chase.

I took a deep breath. "It's not your business," I repeated over and over again, like a mantra. "It's not your business."

It wasn't.

It really wasn't.

Of course, I'd never look.

"What kind of person would I be?" I grimaced and turned my back on the painting.

Exert self-control, Laurie. You can do it.

The trouble was I had the feeling that whatever that folder contained, Chase would probably not tell me, and I wasn't the sort of person who could easily forget the call. Now that I had found the folder, I couldn't move on without looking.

No one would ever hide something, unless they didn't want you to stumble upon it.

I pulled out the brown folder.

It looked plain and harmless. Maybe it was a message from Clint.

My stepfather had been psycho enough to warn us. Maybe he had tried to scare Chase, and Chase being Chase didn't want to worry me.

My fingers traced the contours of the coarse paper,

fighting with my self. In the end I decided to peer inside.

You'd better be right about Clint—because anything else was a violation of Chase's privacy.

My hands shook as I opened the folder, frowning ever so lightly when I noticed how heavy it was. The first thing that stood out was that most of the papers were stapled together, and how used they looked—as if someone had worked with them for a long time.

I read the sticky note attached to the first page where someone had written a message in hurried cursive:

Kade,

You said this was urgent. Have a look and tell me what you want me to do, then return this.

My brows knit in confusion.

Kade?

I knew no one by that name, and Chase had never mentioned him. Maybe someone dropped off the envelope by mistake because that Kade person wasn't staying in our suite.

I should have pushed the papers back inside the folder and returned it to its place, but for some reason I didn't.

After another peek behind me, I began flicking through the papers. There were thirty at least, and two photos of me. One was a headshot and the other seemed to have been taken through a window of a public place I recognized as the coffee shop around the block from where I sometimes grabbed a cup on my way out. Somewhere at the back of my mind alarm bells went off.

"What the hell," I muttered staring at my own face.

I could feel the onset of panic and helplessness.

Was Clint harassing Chase?

That would be so much like him.

I began to read through the pages in the hope of finding a reasonable explanation.

When I reached the third page, my heart stopped in my chest, and cold sweat coated my back. It was a printout of a forwarded email application to LiveInvent Designs and the personal assistant's invitation to come in for an interview with the exact time and date he'd expect me.

It was the day I got stuck in an elevator.

It was the day the floor collapsed; the day I met Mystery Guy.

Somewhere in the distant back of my mind, Chase's voice echoed:

You don't look okay. Do you want to take the stairs?

You're hyperventilating, Laurie.

Breathe, Laurie. You need to breathe.

And just recently:

Being afraid of a lift or of darkness is just human.

A shaky breath escaped my trembling lips as realization

slowly dawned on me.

I had never told Chase about my fear of darkness. I was pretty sure about that.

It was as if he somehow knew that I was afraid of all tight places, especially those devoid of light. His voice had seemed familiar, but I could never quite place it.

It was as if he had been inside that building with me, experiencing that dreadful day.

Maybe he had been.

For the past three months, I had been obsessed with him—the man who had saved my life. I had scanned newspapers, but found no clues, no missing person reports—nothing to indicate he had ever existed, or that he might be missed. It turned out I never had to look very far. Turned out he had been right beside me for a while.

Sure I had noticed some similarities, but with each passing day, the shock, the fear, the trauma, my memories became a blurry mess with just that one kiss vivid in my mind.

I had no idea what to make of the folder in my hands.

Could it still be a big, fat coincidence?

Are you for real?

Obviously, I could ask Chase if he was Mystery Guy but even if I wanted to, that wasn't an option. Not when I sensed he'd be lying.

I closed my eyes and took deep breaths to calm the

nausea rising in my stomach.

Something was wrong. Very wrong. I could feel it in my bones.

I knew that feeling. It was the same one I had felt before my mother's mental breakdown.

That same dark energy was here, beckoning to me to get to the truth of the matter, while pushing me away at the same.

Don't go there.

Keep on the blindfold.

Stay in the dark.

Opening my eyes, I took a deep breath and released it slowly when I noticed that one sheet of paper had slipped out. I lifted it off the floor and began to read. Even though it was only a four-line paragraph printout, my world stopped spinning.

Not interested in her life story. Just send over the details of her will and a copy of her bank statements as well as an estimate how much the estate's worth.

Sincerely,

Kade Wright

My eyes stopped at the last two words.

Kade Wright.

Not Chase.

Kade.

What the fuck?

"Son of a bitch."

The bottom of my stomach dropped, and I sank down to the floor in shock, my fingers gripping the folder so tightly I feared I might just tear it in half. A soft cry escaped my lips, and a tear rolled down my cheek, followed by another, and another, until they formed a steady stream. I wiped at them angrily, suddenly understanding why Chase once said:

Give me just one night so I can forget you.

He had never wanted to help me. Never intended to stay with me.

It had been a ploy.

It was all about Waterfront Shore.

He wanted my mother's money.

When I entrusted Mystery Guy with my secrets, I assumed they'd be buried forever. Chase had seemed familiar right from the beginning, but it never occurred to me that he might be the guy from the elevator. Worse than that, Chase harbored secrets of his own.

He wasn't just the keeper of my secrets; he was hiding his own from me. What I thought had been goodwill on his part didn't sound so random after all.

Suddenly, my worst fears began to take shape and

morph into one scary conclusion. I had been targeted. It had all been a carefully executed plan. Or maybe it all started harmless enough but as soon as he discovered who I was, he used all the information he had on me to stage a meeting. That had to be the case, because I couldn't possibly imagine someone would be responsible for a whole floor crashing to get my trust. Only, I never considered the possibility that I might fall in love with him.

A soft sob escaped my throat.

The pain I felt in my heart was ripping. It went through every layer of my skin, tearing, splitting—burning everything in its wake.

It was all a lie, Laurie. The whole 'I'm into you' was.

And I couldn't believe I had been so stupid as to sleep with him. That I had broken the one major promise I had made to myself and trusted him enough to open up my heart and body.

Damn Chase. Or whatever his name was.

Damn me for falling and trusting when my past should have taught me better than that.

And damn me for being so utterly, irrevocably stupid as to fall in love with a man like him.

The previous night had been the calm before the storm. Now the storm was raging, surging through me, cutting my heart like a knife and splitting it into two. If I could have ripped out my heart to make it stop bleeding, I would have taken the knife and plunged it deep into me.

Who was this guy?

Because Chase didn't exist.

Did I ever really know him? Probably not, because it all boiled down to one fact: Chase's name was Kade and this whole marriage thing was a big sham based on a false identity and probably lots of other lies. When I had agreed to marry him it didn't say in the brochure that he was a lying bastard.

The suspicion had been there all along, growing in my heart the moment the seed of doubt was planted, but the knowledge didn't make it hurt any less.

Whatever Chase's reasons were, I had been deceived. Lied to.

And now I had to get away—from him, from it all, from everything—before he woke up.

I had to escape to some place where no one could find me; where no one would witness my shame at being so stupid.

Years ago I had promised myself I'd stop running, but running was the one thing that kept saving me.

Hot tears streamed down my cheeks as I stormed for my room, not even closing the door as I grabbed clean underwear, a pair of jeans and a shirt from the closet and changed into them, barely paying attention to the stunning wedding gown I had worn the day before.

The day I had made the biggest mistake of my life.

The day I had gifted my trust and body to the one guy who most certainly didn't deserve it.

Another small cry escaped my lips as I closed my eyes, wishing for once that I had never taken that phone call. If I hadn't found the folder, I would still be in my blissful state, and we'd have a good time.

Ignoring the rest of my stuff, I stashed my cell phone and passport into my handbag, ready to leave the country— far, far away from him.

Before I stepped out, I glanced back at the note I left on the table along with my wedding ring and the folder:

You're a liar, Kade, and I hope you'll rot in hell.

Somewhere behind me, a door opened. I knew it was Chase, his perfect half naked body emerging in search of me.

His voice carried over. "Laurie?"

With tears streaming down my face, I closed the door quietly, then started to run. I had probably never run faster in my life.

Meeting Chase had been too good to be true.

Chase had been nothing but wishful thinking.

It had been too easy, and I had been too naïve to see it.

Chase had been so unbelievably good in pretending. His

concern for me had been touching that it was believably easy for me to fall for his lies. Now I was getting hit by the truth in the worst possible way and paying the price.

But I wasn't going to let him shatter me; I wasn't going to let anyone keep me from getting my mother's letters. Not when I had worked so hard to get them.

"Where do you want to go?" the driver asked impatiently.

I stared at him in shock, unsure to do or say.

"To the airport, please," I whispered eventually, wrapping my arms around my waist as I realized I didn't even have a jacket.

Then I'd make sure to leave for a place where I wouldn't need one.

Seven days.

That's how long I'd have to stay married to him to get them—the one thing that meant the most to me.

He had hurt me, but I'd do whatever I could to move on. Fly away. If I got away real fast, real far, I had every hope, every faith that I could outrun both Chase Wright and the pain lodged deep in my heart.

I might have let a guy, thief that he was, get under my skin and steal my trust, but at least I still had my old life. I had me. I had a best friend. That surely counted for something.

Soon, I'd also have my mother's letters. I'd uncover her

secrets.

With or without Chase, or Kade, or whoever he was.

*** The End…for now***

*An Indecent Proposal: The Agreement
continues in the sensual conclusion,*

An Indecent

Proposal:

BAD BOY

COMING FEB. 23RD, 2016

Please join our mailing list to be notified of the release:

http://jcreedauthor.blogspot.com/p/mailing-list.html

http://authorjackiesteele.blogspot.com/p/subscribe.html

If you enjoyed this book, please leave a review, as they are hard to come by for indie authors. And finally, don't be a stranger. We love to hear from our readers and always write back. To contact us, visit the blogs above or join us on Facebook (links are on the next page.)

ABOUT THE AUTHORS

Jackie S. Steele has lived most of her life in New England. She never read a book she didn't like. Her love for books began when she stumbled upon her mother's secret dash of Harlequin books, and couldn't stop reading until she had finished them all. Today she still loves curling up with a good book, sipping coffee, and taking long walks on the beach.

http://www.facebook.com/AuthorJackieSteele

http://jackiesteele.wix.com/main

J.C. Reed is the multiple New York Times, Wall Street Journal and USA Today bestselling author of SURRENDER YOUR LOVE and NO EXCEPTIONS. She writes steamy contemporary fiction with a touch of mystery. When she's not typing away on her keyboard, forgetting the world around her, she dreams of returning to the beautiful mountains of Wyoming. You can also find her chatting on Facebook with her readers or spending time with her children.

https://www.facebook.com/AuthorJCReed

http://jcreedauthor.blogspot.com

BOOKS BY J.C. REED:

SURRENDER YOUR LOVE
CONQUER YOUR LOVE
TREASURE YOUR LOVE
THE LOVER'S SECRET
THE LOVER'S GAME
THE LOVER'S PROMISE
THE LOVER'S SURRENDER
THAT GUY
AN INDECENT PROPOSAL: THE INTERVIEW
AN INDECENT PROPOSAL: THE AGREEMENT

BOOKS BY JACKIE STEELE:

THAT GUY
AN INDECENT PROPOSAL: THE INTERVIEW
AN INDECENT PROPOSAL: THE *AGREEMENT*

Made in the USA
San Bernardino, CA
09 July 2017